FRANKENSTEIN DARCY

Pride and Prejudice Paranormal

Cass Grix

Cover design by beetifulbookcovers.com
Cover image by MaxFrost/stock.adobe.com
Formatting by Polgarus Studio

Website: www.cassgrix.com
Facebook: www.facebook.com/Cass-Grix-1271639419512755/
Email: cass.grix.author@gmail.com
Mailing list: www.cassgrix.com

CHAPTER ONE

1804

Lizzy Bennet had seen enough portraits and chairs to last a lifetime.

Unlike her older sister Jane who almost swooned over fine carpets and satin curtains, Lizzy preferred nature to the ornate accomplishments of men. When her Aunt and Uncle Gardiner had invited them to tour Derbyshire, Lizzy had been looking forward to seeing new landscapes. As a young girl of thirteen, she had seen little of the world beyond her home in Hertfordshire and she was eager to travel.

But she had been taught her manners, so she smiled and tried not to look as bored as she felt when they toured yet another beautiful home: Pemberley, owned by the Darcy family.

They were in the area because her aunt had spent

some of her youth in Lambton, a small town near Pemberley. They had come for Mrs. Gardiner to visit with old friends, and Mr. Gardiner wanted to see Pemberley. "I have heard they have some of the finest woods in the country."

As they walked through the house, Lizzy kept looking out the windows rather than at the furnishings. From the dining parlour she saw a hill, crowned with wood, from which they had approached the large house. She sighed with pleasure. It was a beautiful view. She admired the whole scene: the river, the trees scattered on its banks, and the winding of the valley, as far as she could trace it. She sighed with delight.

She thought that if she had been fortunate enough to live here, she would have spent her days out of doors, exploring the grounds.

The housekeeper, a pleasant elderly woman, gave the tour.

In one sitting room, Mrs. Gardiner noticed a collection of miniatures over the mantelpiece. "Mrs. Reynolds," she asked. "Is this young man the son of Master Darcy? If so, he has the look of his father."

"Oh, do you know the Master?" the housekeeper asked.

"I met him and Lady Anne in Lambton years ago,

but I do not know them."

Mrs. Reynolds said, "Yes, the gentleman on the left is Mr. Frankenstein Darcy. The gentleman on the right is the son of the Master's steward."

"Both handsome young men," Mrs. Gardiner said with approval.

Lizzy looked closer at the miniatures, not impressed. They were handsome portraits, but even her neighbour Sir William Lucas had a handsome portrait of himself hanging in his drawing room. The artist had corrected all his flaws and painted him as if he were twenty years younger and two stone lighter.

"And here is a recent portrait of Miss Darcy."

Lizzy looked at the portrait of a young girl in a pretty pink dress. She looked about the age of her younger sister Lydia.

"Frankenstein," Mr. Gardiner said, musing. "Is that a German name?"

"No, Genevan," Mrs. Reynolds answered. "It is a family name. The young Master is called Frankenstein for his father's family, then Fitzwilliam for his mother's."

"Frankenstein Fitzwilliam Darcy," Lizzy whispered to Jane. "It must have taken a long time to learn to write it." She was glad that her name was much simpler.

"I have always thought it a nice custom to name one's children family names," Mrs. Gardiner said to the housekeeper. "It gives a child something to aspire to."

"I agree," Mrs. Reynolds said. "And there is no better master than Mr. Darcy. He is the best landlord, so affable to the poor and needy. You might not have noticed, but some of the servants at Pemberley are maimed. Unlike many wealthy men who require their staff to be physically beautiful, Mr. Darcy is more concerned for their characters and their willingness to work. He has hired many who are crippled or otherwise injured. Indeed, his valet Greenwood is a hideous man but has a heart of gold." She turned to Lizzy and Jane. "Some children are frightened by him, thinking he is a monster, but you are old enough to know better."

Jane's heart was touched by his plight. "The poor man," she murmured. "I hope I would see the good man inside regardless of his outer appearance."

Lizzy smiled. Jane always saw the good in others.

When all the house that was open to general inspection had been seen, they returned downstairs and, taking leave of the housekeeper, were consigned over to the gardener, who met them at the hall door.

Mr. Gardiner spoke to the gardener about the date of

the building and various modifications. Mrs. Gardiner was interested in the rose gardens and the vegetable gardens. The gardener mentioned two different walks available in the park – one that was two miles and a larger of ten miles. Lizzy wished they could take the ten mile walk but knew that would be beyond her aunt's capacity. "May we go on the shorter walk?" she asked.

Mrs. Gardiner declined. "I am too tired. I would rather sit by the roses. What of you, Mr. Gardiner?"

He turned to the servant. "Is the shorter walk well defined?"

"Yes, sir. It walks by the side of a pond and through some woods."

"Have any of your guests gotten lost before?"

"None that I know of."

"Very well," Mr. Gardiner said. "Lizzy, Jane you make take the shorter walk if you wish. I will stay with your aunt."

Lizzy caught his hand and kissed it. "Oh, thank you, sir."

He laughed at her exuberance. "But don't dawdle too much or wander off. If it takes you more than an hour, I will come after you."

"I will keep her on the path," Jane said seriously.

"You are both good girls," Mr. Gardiner said. "Run along."

Lizzy would like to run, but she knew Jane would not. "Hurry, Jane," she urged.

The gardener showed them where the path began and explained that it turned left, past a pond, up a slight hill and then down again, where they would ultimately see the west side of the house and the stables.

Lizzy could not wait. Once they were out of sight of her aunt and uncle she took off her bonnet and ran her fingers through her hair, dislodging the ribbon that tied it back.

"Lizzy," Jane said with gentle disapproval.

"Don't worry," Lizzy said. She wound the ribbon around her fingers and then stuffed it in her pocket. "I will keep my bonnet around my neck and tie up my hair before we return." She sighed. "If I had my way, I would never wear a bonnet again."

"Or shoes," Jane teased. "Sometimes I think Papa is right and you are a natural savage."

Lizzy held her arms out wide and looked up into the bright blue sky. She felt the sun warm on her face. "How can anyone bear to be cooped up in a house on such a glorious day? I thought we would never leave."

"I thought Pemberley was a very pretty house."

"It is," Lizzy agreed. "But I am more interested in rocks and trees."

"And dirt."

Lizzy looked at her sister. When they were younger, she and Jane had both played in the yard at Longbourn, making little houses out of twigs and leaves, but in the past two years, Jane had grown into a woman. She had started her courses and now had a lovely feminine figure. Their mother said she was sure to catch a wealthy husband someday.

Lizzy's body was starting to change as well, and she did not look forward to the transformation. She had always felt strong and capable as a child. Indeed, her father had often treated her as if she were a boy, teaching her chess and letting her read everything in his library. But now, as her breasts were beginning to grow and her waist was narrowing, she felt ugly and awkward. She dreaded having a bosom as large as her mother. She knew breasts were biologically necessary, but right now, they seemed inconvenient.

Together she and Jane walked by the side of a large pond. Every step brought them to a nobler fall of ground or a finer reach of the woods. Jane wore a women's white dress with a contrasting navy pelisse. Elizabeth's dress was simpler – a light brown with accents of white at the throat. It was also shorter, displaying at the hem several inches of her decorative pantalettes, which proclaimed her youth and also gave her a little more room for taking longer strides when she walked. But as her mother often reminded her, "Just because you can be a hoyden, doesn't mean you should."

Lizzy walked quickly, invigorated by the fresh air and the beauty of her surroundings. At one point, Jane asked Lizzy to stop so she could remove a pebble from her shoe. As Lizzy waited for her sister to untie her boot, she looked along the shoreline for a good rock. She found several small stones that were smooth and flat and had a nice heft to them – not too heavy or they would sink, but substantial enough to make a nice skip along the water's surface as she threw them. Her father preferred circular rocks, but she liked a rock with a slight triangular shape. She held one in her hand, resting the flat sides of the rock between her thumb and the tip of her middle finger. She hugged the flat edge of the stone with her index finger. She twisted her hand so that the rock was almost parallel to the ground, pulled her arm back and with a flick of her wrist, sent the stone skimming across the surface. "Look at that, Jane," she said happily. "Four hops."

Jane, having retied her boot, brushed her skirts down. "I did not see it."

"No bother," Lizzy said. "I will try again." She took the second stone and flicked her wrist. This time the stone hopped six times before sinking to the bottom of the pond.

"Very nice," Jane said, just as they heard someone clapping.

Lizzy turned to see a tall young man, possibly twenty years of age with brown hair, wearing a damp white shirt and tan breeches, approach them. His legs were bare, with a few blades of grass sticking to them.

"An excellent boy's trick," he said. "I congratulate you, miss."

Jane gasped.

Lizzy said irritably, "It is not a boy's trick if a girl has thrown it."

"I stand corrected," he said formally and made an elegant bow. "Please forgive the interference, but I had been swimming and did not want to alarm you by following you back to the house."

Lizzy saw that his hair was dripping and the shirt clung to his trim but muscled chest. His shirt was open, without a cravat and there was an angry red scar across his throat, as if it had been cut and then hastily stitched closed.

She swallowed nervously at the gruesome sight. "You are?"

"Frank Darcy," he said pleasantly. "And I assume you are touring the house." He spoke with confidence as a well-educated, wealthy young man. Lizzy recognized him as the heir to Pemberley.

"Yes." They both nodded.

"Do you like it?"

"Yes, very much," Jane said politely.

"I like your woods," Lizzy volunteered.

He smiled. "So do I. Whenever I am away from Pemberley, I long to return."

Jane said, "We are touring with our aunt and uncle. They are waiting for us." Lizzy could tell that Jane was uncomfortable by their conversation and thought it best to turn back.

"Then I will not delay you. If you would like, I can escort you, unless you consider that a presumption."

Lizzy snorted. "The path is the path. What is the point of your waiting half an hour to give us privacy?" Sometimes society's rules were ridiculous. She knew from Jane's wide eyes and frown that she would not want Lizzy to give him their names because they had not been introduced yet. But it wasn't as if they were all dressed up and facing each other in a ballroom. "My name is Lizzy," she said bluntly. "And this is my sister Jane."

Jane glared at her, but Lizzy ignored that. At least she had not given the young man their last name.

"Very good," he said. "Let me retrieve my boots and I will accompany you."

He stepped back to an area that was more heavily wooded. Lizzy heard a rustling sound and then two shots rang out, close together.

"Mr. Darcy?" she called.

She heard a groan.

Lizzy stepped towards the woods as she heard the sound of someone else running.

Jane caught her arm. "Lizzy, no. What if the man who fired the shots is still there?"

Lizzy tugged her arm free. "He may be hurt."

She found the young Mr. Darcy lying on his back, his hands on his lower abdomen. Bright red blood seeped through his clothes and his fingers. Lizzy had never seen so much blood. She looked around, and saw a man in the distance with a battered hat and worn clothes running away.

"Jane, come help me!" she cried.

"No," Darcy said as he searched her face. "Hurry back to the house. I don't want you to be in danger as well."

"Can you walk?" Lizzy asked.

He closed his eyes, grimacing from the pain. "No."

"Then I will go get help."

"I am losing a lot of blood. There might not be enough time."

"Don't say that," Lizzy argued.

Jane approached, clutching her hands before herself in distress. "What can we do?"

Lizzy said, "I don't know."

"Staunch the bleeding," Darcy said weakly.

"With what?" Lizzy said.

"My shirt? Fold it up and press it on the wounds."

There was no way she would be able to help him remove his shirt. Instead she loosened and stepped out of her pantalettes.

"Lizzy!" Jane exclaimed, horrified.

She handed them to Jane. "It doesn't matter. I still have petticoats. Do what he says." Jane nervously folded the white fabric and put it over his wounds.

"Press down," Darcy ordered.

Jane did so but winced. "I don't want to hurt you."

"Too late," Darcy said.

For a second, Lizzy thought he was saying that it was too late and that he was dying, but then she realized he meant that Jane would hurt him, regardless.

Lizzy said, "Stay with him and I will run back to the house and tell the servants." She leaned closer to the young man. "I don't know how far we walked. Which way is closer to the house – left or right?"

He pointed. "West."

"Don't die," she thought desperately, "Please don't die."

She must have spoken out loud for he smiled grimly and said, "I will try not to."

Lizzy lifted up her skirts, baring her calves, and ran a mile back to Pemberley, stopping only when her breath required it. She came into the rose garden, shouting, "Help! Help! There has been an accident!"

Mr. Gardiner seeing the blood on her dress and lack of bonnet cried out, "Lizzy, have you been hurt?"

"No, sir," she said quickly, leaning forward slightly, her hands on her knees as she gasped for breath. "It is the young master of the house. He has been shot."

"Shot? But how? Hunting season hasn't started."

"I don't know," Lizzy said. "He was on the path by the pond. He was shot twice and is bleeding out."

Mrs. Gardiner turned to the gardener. "A carriage or cart perhaps?"

The gardener ran to the stables and in a few minutes, a cart and several single men on horses were riding down the walking path.

Lizzy wished that she could go with them, but knew she would only be in the way. "Lizzy," Mrs. Gardiner said with admiration. "How brave you are."

Lizzy did not feel brave. She felt sick with fear, and now that she had nothing else she must do, she started shaking.

"It was so sudden," she said. "He was talking with us and

the next moment he was shot." It was incomprehensible to her that someone could be so vibrant and alive one moment and a minute later, be struggling to live.

"Shh," Mrs. Gardiner crooned. "They will send for a doctor. He will get the care he needs."

Lizzy clung to her and cried.

Half an hour later, the men returned with the young Mr. Darcy carried on a wooden pallet covered with blankets. He was still and unmoving as if he had passed out from the pain and loss of blood. Jane was there as well. She had ridden on someone's horse. She was returned to Mrs. Gardiner. She also cried, and Mrs. Gardiner handed her a handkerchief. Jane said, "He told me to tell his parents that he loved them and then he stopped talking and did not open his eyes."

Mrs. Gardiner nodded and patted her arm. "You can write a letter to Mrs. Darcy tomorrow and tell her that. I am certain she would like to hear it and will not mind the impropriety of your writing to someone you do not know."

"Yes, ma'am," Jane said.

Mr. Gardiner had gone over to where the servants were carrying the young man to see how bad the situation was and to offer his assistance. He saw the young Mr. Darcy briefly before he was carried inside the house.

When he returned to his wife and nieces, his face was solemn.

"I do hope he will recover," Jane said.

Lizzy saw the quick glance Mr. Gardiner gave Mrs. Gardiner and she knew that the young man was dead.

CHAPTER TWO

1806 – TWO YEARS LATER

Frankenstein Darcy left London and returned to Pemberley as soon as he heard of his father's illness. He rode straight through, stopping only to change horses and arrived late in the evening.

The letter stated that his father had been ill for several weeks but had not wanted to bother him. He did not want to interrupt his son's studies for a matter that would no doubt be cured by ample rest and sensible eating.

But when Mr. George Darcy was unable to communicate and seemed to be succumbing to a fever, Mrs. Reynolds intervened and informed Darcy that his father was too ill to ask him to come.

Darcy left his horse in the stables and hurried into the house. He handed his hat and gloves to a footman and took the stairs two at a time to get to the master bedroom.

His father was pale and lay on the large canopy bed with the curtains tied back.

"Father!" Darcy cried. His father stirred but his eyes did not open.

Darcy put his hand to his father's face. Hot and damp. He had a fever.

"What has been done for him?" he demanded.

A woman, one of the servants, sitting beside him said, "He refused to send for a doctor, sir. You know how he is."

Yes, Darcy knew. His father was an amateur scientist who prided himself on his medical skills. He thought most doctors were barbarians. He often said, "Fools, ninety-five percent of them. They know nothing of how to preserve life. Let alone create it. Why should I let them physic me when I can do better myself?"

"Has he had anything to eat or drink?"

"Yarrow tea this morning."

Darcy nodded. That could help. He opened his father's shirt and placed his ear on his chest to listen to his breathing. Shallow and troubled. "Get me steam," he told the servant. "And herbs: thyme and sage. And make up a peppermint salve if there is none available."

"Yes, sir."

In the middle of the night, his father spoke. "Frankenstein?"

His father never shortened his name, as most of his acquaintances did. "Sir?" Darcy said, approaching him. "Are you better now?"

"No, I am dying."

"Do you want me to fetch a doctor?" They were the only two people in the room, but he could wake the footman sitting on a bench in the hallway.

His father laughed weakly. "No, they would only want to bleed me and send me to my Maker a few hours earlier." His breath was laboured and speaking took a great effort. His words were slow but deliberate.

"Surely there is something I can do."

"Besides rubbing me down with peppermint oil? I recognize your signature fragrance."

Darcy smiled. It was one of their common topics of conversation. His father was more interested in surgery than herbs and he thought Darcy's praise of the virtues of peppermint excessive.

His father took a deep, shuddering breath.

"I wish you had sent for me earlier," Darcy said.

"Waste of time. No, don't glare at me. I have lived a good life. And I look forward to seeing your mother. If she has forgiven me."

"Forgiven?"

His father shook his head. "Too many times I put my wants above hers. I loved her dearly, but she had reason to resent me. And one more reason, for I will now do what she begged me not to do."

Darcy frowned. His father had rarely spoken about his mother, as if it had been too painful to talk about her after her death.

His father said, "Take my necklace." He always wore a chain around his neck that held a key.

Darcy removed the necklace. "Do you want me to open a door for you?"

"Yes. To my private laboratory."

When Darcy was a child, he had often played in his father's laboratory. He had been fascinated by his father's dissection of animals and his study of electricity. But by the time he was twelve, he came home from school to find the laboratory locked. When he asked about it, his father said, "Some study is not for children."

Darcy had been offended that his father did not trust him, but as an obedient son, he accepted his rule without question.

Over the years since then, there had been rumours that his father was conducting experiments in human dissection as well as animal. There were whispers about grave robbing. But Mr. Darcy, as Master of Pemberley and a local magistrate, was well respected throughout Derbyshire and no criminal accusations had ever been made.

Darcy held the key in his hand. Finally, he would be able to know the truth.

His father said, "It is your laboratory now, if you want it. As Master of Pemberley, you should have all the keys."

Darcy protested. "Not Master, yet. You can get well, I know it."

His father smiled briefly. "But son, I don't want to get well." Every sentence was difficult for him, but he persevered and Darcy leaned closer to be able to hear him. "I am not a perfect man. In my pride and conceit, I have sinned before God, but in His mercy, I hope to rest. I have made my peace with Him. Take care of your sister."

Georgiana. In his concern for his father, Darcy had not thought of her. "Is she here?"

His father nodded. "Upstairs. Asleep. I have spoken with her. She is a good girl."

His father suffered another painful spasm and did not speak for several minutes. Darcy took his hand. "I don't want you to die."

His father gathered his strength to whisper, "You

are a good man, the best son I could have ever wanted." At this his father closed his eyes and did not speak.

Darcy held onto his hand, feeling his pulse, wishing there was something more he could do to make his father well. He was not ready to be Master of Pemberley. He was too young, too inexperienced. And how could he take care of Georgiana, become her only parent? It was much too soon for his father to die.

For an hour, his father said nothing, too weak to do more than moan or stir in his bed. Then his father suddenly opened his eyes and said, "Wickham."

"What of him?" George Wickham was the son of his father's steward. They were of an age, having been born only four months apart, himself the senior. They had met when they were five and had grown up together on the estate. At one time they had been friends, but Darcy did not like him now.

His father said slowly, "Wish I could see him. Marvellous young man."

His father did not know Wickham and his vices, and Darcy would not distress him by outlining them now.

His father closed his eyes again. "Take care of him."

"You have been more than generous to him," Darcy said. His father had paid for Wickham's education and had often sent him money. Money that Wickham wasted on riotous living: drinking, gambling and whoring.

"You don't understand." His father coughed for a minute, and when he spoke again, his words were so faint, they were difficult to discern. "Second son to me. My responsibility and now yours."

Darcy could not believe what he was hearing. Was Wickham his father's bastard? They bore the same first name, but Darcy had thought that a coincidence. His father had always had a soft spot for him. But had he slept with his steward's wife? The thought made him want to vomit.

Especially when his own mother had been a saint: beautiful, intelligent, and kind, and Wickham's mother had been coarse, fat, and unlettered. She had died when he and Wickham were children.

Darcy said carefully, "Is George Wickham your son?"

His father sighed and when he looked in Darcy's eyes, Darcy saw pain, guilt and remorse. He moved his head as if nodding. "For my sins."

"Damn you," Darcy said fiercely and turned away. He knew people told the truth on their deathbeds, but at that moment he wished his father had died before he came home. He wished his father were dead and buried so he would not have to know what kind of man he truly was. He felt as if the man lying in the bed had just murdered his father – his true father, the man he had almost worshiped as a child.

He left the room, too angry to speak. The motion woke the liveried footman who was sitting on a bench outside the door. "Sir?" the young man asked.

"Go sit with the master," Darcy ordered. As he walked quickly to the library, he heard his father call out, "Frankenstein!" but he did not turn back.

* * *

The morning light was like a dagger in his eye straight through to his brain. Darcy rubbed his face and groaned. It had been years since he had drunk whiskey on an empty stomach, but he recognized the signs.

Gradually he became aware of his surroundings. He was in the library, sprawled out on one of the couches. His coat and waistcoat on the floor. Cravat somewhere. He sat up, loosely remembering the events of the night before.

His father dying. Telling him about Wickham.

He winced. Heavens, what a blow. Wickham his half-brother? No wonder he had drunk too much.

And his father? What of him?

Now, in the miserable light of day, with a throbbing headache, Darcy was more sympathetic to the sins of the flesh. Perhaps it had just been a weak moment. Could he forgive a man for a mistake made more than twenty years before?

In his favour, his father had tried to make amends by providing for Wickham. Darcy wondered if Wickham Senior had known the truth, that he had been hired as steward because of his wife's child.

In addition, George Darcy had devoted years of his life to charitable works, possibly as a penance.

As much as Darcy hated what his father had done in siring Wickham, he was not a complete villain.

He himself had said he was not a perfect man, that he had sinned against God.

And who had not?

Darcy had his own flaws – a resentful temper being one of them.

He sighed. He would go upstairs and apologize to his father. For whatever his father's sins were, he should not have damned him. The state of his eternal soul was a matter between him and his Maker - no one else. Darcy, as his son, must do his duty and honour him.

He stood on shaky legs.

Georgiana entered the room, her eyes and face red with tears. She was taller than he remembered but still a child, only ten years of age. "Frank?" she called out.

"Have you heard? Father is dead."

Darcy held his arms open and she embraced him and cried.

His father was dead.

Darcy clenched his teeth. Death had robbed him of his chance to apologize. That meant his harsh words to his father were the last ones he heard. He had been unable to tell his mother that he loved her before her death, and now it was the same with his father.

No human being could have passed a happier childhood than himself. His parents were possessed by the very spirit of kindness and indulgence. He never felt that they were tyrants, ruling over their lot according to caprice, but instead they were the agents and creators of all the many delights that he had enjoyed. Especially his father, who had introduced him to the joys of science.

And how had he rewarded him? With anger and disrespect.

Regret tasted bitter in his mouth.

"What will become of us?" Georgiana asked, finally letting him go and stepping back. "With no father and no mother?"

"I will take care of you," Darcy promised.

"But what of your college? Your studies?"

"I will take care of you and Pemberley," he said. "My studies can wait."

* * *

The next few weeks were long and arduous, first with his father's funeral and meeting with his solicitors. Surprisingly, his father's steward's health was also poor, a heart condition, and he died within days of his father's death. Although it was inconvenient to hire a new steward, Darcy was relieved because he had dreaded speaking to the man he had always thought was Wickham's father.

His father's will provided a one-thousand-pound legacy for Wickham and a request that if he took orders, for him to be given a valuable living as soon as it became vacant.

"Is that all?" Wickham asked when Darcy gave him the money. "I had hoped for more."

Wickham was expensively dressed with a vividly embroidered waistcoat. His cravat was starched and tied in a complicated pattern. The chain for his watch was jewelled. One thousand pounds would not last long in his pocket, Darcy thought.

He looked deep into Wickham's eyes, wondering if he knew his true parentage. But he would not tell him if he did not know already. The last thing he wanted was Wickham deciding that he deserved even more from the estate.

"A clergyman?" Wickham asked and laughed. "Can you see me giving sermons?"

"No, I cannot."

"Well then, why don't you make an exchange? I am thinking of studying the law, which would be a better match for my talents, don't you think?"

"I think you have a better chance of needing lawyers in your life rather than becoming one."

"Oh, I am much more careful than I was when I was younger."

"No longer trying to kill people in drunken rages?" Darcy asked. Wickham had a quick temper, often lashing out. Later, he would be sorry and apologetic. There had been several incidents when they were at college that his father's generosity had helped to diminish.

"Trust me, the next time I want to kill someone, I will do it cold stone sober."

Darcy shivered. Was that a threat? He knew Wickham hated him. As a child, he had resented the fact that an accident of birth made Darcy an heir to a vast estate. It is not fair, he often said. Why should you be so blessed? Are we not both equal before God? Why could we not have the same advantages?

Darcy said, "Let me speak to my solicitors and I will write back to you."

"My address," Wickham said with a flourish and handed him a professionally printed card.

Darcy glanced at the address. Wickham was definitely living beyond his means. "Thank you."

Two months later, Darcy approached Mrs. Reynolds. "I am going to open my father's laboratory. Later today, I will need to have several maids, possibly a footman to tidy it."

"That won't be necessary, sir."

"I beg your pardon?"

"The laboratory is as clean as the rest of Pemberley. I run an efficient household, Mr. Darcy."

"Are you telling me that you have seen inside the laboratory?" It would be doubly offensive if he had not been allowed inside for years when the housekeeper had.

"Oh no, not I," she said with a nervous laugh. "The old Master would have had apoplexy, to be sure. No, Greenwood takes care of it. He always has."

Greenwood was his father's valet, a large, silent, scarred man. "How could he clean it when I have the key?"

"Greenwood has his own key, sir."

Darcy was astonished, but decided that it was another aspect of his father's character that he might never understand. Perhaps he had thought that Greenwood, a mute, would never divulge his secrets. "Very well, Mrs. Reynolds. Please have Greenwood report to me."

In a few minutes, Greenwood joined him. He stood formally, bowed his head, and gave a grunt that Darcy assumed meant "sir."

Greenwood's face was ugly with deep, puckered scars across his forehead and down one cheek, but time and familiarity had reduced Darcy's natural horror. "Greenwood, I understand that you have a key to my father's laboratory."

The large man nodded.

"May I see it?"

He unbuttoned his shirt with massive fingers and showed a chain and key identical to Darcy's own.

Darcy said, "All right then, you shall accompany me."

Together they walked downstairs, through Pemberley's basement, past the wine cellar. The door to the laboratory was thick, dark wood. Darcy used his own key to unlock it. He hesitated a moment before opening the door. He had waited eleven years for this day, but he had delayed it for two months, not certain he was ready to learn more of his father's secrets.

But he would rather know the truth than be afraid of the shadows, so he pushed the door open.

The laboratory was as he remembered: a large, surprisingly bright room with natural light from dozens of windows just above ground level that ringed the ceiling. There were three large tables in the centre of the room and several unnaturally high seated chairs, so a man could sit comfortably at the table rather than standing to work. The wall to the left contained two sinks and cabinets with glass doors. The cabinets were filled with bottles and equipment. There was a large collection of knives, scissors, plyers and saws.

He remembered as a child watching his father saw open the head of a horse to examine its brain and spinal column. Darcy had been fascinated rather than repulsed and his father had explained all the different parts of the body and how they worked together.

Over the years, he had watched his father dissect many different species. He had also seen him stitch up several people at Pemberley when there was an injury. Indeed, his father had performed the surgery on his abdomen when he was shot two years before and done an excellent job.

Were the rumours correct and had his father dissected humans as well? That was illegal, but many medical students paid Resurrection Men to obtain bodies.

Darcy opened several cupboards and a large trunk, fearing what he might discover, but fortunately for his peace of mind, there were no cadavers in the laboratory – and very little dust. Greenwood was an excellent housekeeper.

The back wall of the laboratory contained bookcases and to the right there was a collection of electrical equipment. The Leyden jar and friction generators were items he remembered, but there was a new contraption, which looked like a large variation of a Voltaic Pile. "Is this my father's invention?" he asked.

Greenwood nodded.

"How do I use it?" Darcy asked.

Greenwood walked over to the bookcases with his halting steps and returned with a bound journal of his father's notes. He flipped through the pages and handed him an open volume. Darcy was fascinated by the detailed drawings and the instructions. "So it stores electricity from lightning?"

Greenwood nodded.

"Genius." Lightning rods had been installed at Pemberley more than fifty years earlier. It was brilliant for his father to devise a way to harness that power. But it was dangerous as well, and he supposed his father hadn't wanted him to get shocked by playing with it without supervision. "Is that it?" he asked.

Greenwood shook his head. He walked slowly over to the bookcase and returned with another bound volume. He opened this book to an entry dated November 3, 1794. Darcy read:

A week ago, there was a robbery at Pemberley. A

foreign traveller was attacked by a group of men. The traveller fought back with an axe, killing two of his assailants, but he was gravely injured. One of his arms and one of his legs were crushed, and he had head wounds as well as a stomach wound.

This was Greenwood. Darcy remembered his father telling him the story when he returned from school. He had been particularly impressed with Greenwood's bravery and skill with the axe. Darcy smiled briefly at Greenwood and continued reading his father's notes.

I did what I could but he died on the table. I looked at the man and wished I could make him whole again, with the principles I had learned from my prior experiments. I knew I could regenerate life. With my electrical apparatus, I possessed the capacity of bestowing animation, but there would be no purpose unless his frame was in a proper form.

His leg and arm were past repair, so I used those of his murderers.

I felt this was a form of justice.

Besides, what use would they have for their limbs? It was not as if I would reanimate them, as well. And the law would not mind if the villains were buried without all their body parts.

In the end, I also replaced one ear and his stomach.

The process was complex, since it involved the intricacies of fibres, muscles and veins, and I had to work quickly, but Praise be to God, it was a success. I felt akin to the Good Samaritan who aided the man who had been set upon by thieves.

I have only two regrets. First is that upon waking, my new Creation had no voice. His throat had been damaged in the attack. If I had known, I might have replaced his vocal cords as well.

Second, I regret that I told my wife of my work. Instead of being proud of my achievement, she was horrified. Lady Anne said I was playing God and using dark arts. I tried to explain that it was merely the application of scientific knowledge, but she was adamantly opposed.

In order to preserve harmony in our marriage, I vowed to conduct no more experiments of this nature.

Darcy closed the book, stunned by what he had read. He was simultaneously amazed and horrified. To think that his father had put together a man and had brought him back to life.

So many events in his own life made sense now, such as Greenwood and his dog-like devotion to his father. He remembered a conversation he'd had with his father years before. He had noticed that one of Greenwood's arms was shorter than the other and had commented on this oddity to his father. His father had said simply, "Good observation and attention to detail."

"But how?" Darcy had asked. "Was he born that way?"

"No. After the accident, there was not as much useable tissue after I made the repairs."

And then there was his mother who had never liked Greenwood. He had never heard her say it specifically, but he had noticed that she would leave a room whenever the large man entered, and she had never referred to him by name.

One time, Darcy had asked his father why he had kept Greenwood on, why he had hired a mute servant. "What else could I do?" his father answered. "His recovery took weeks. He had been robbed of everything he owned. From our rudimentary visual communication, I knew he had no family, no one to return to. I felt responsible for him. Besides, can you imagine how the world would treat him? What would have happened if I had abandoned him? I hate to think of him wandering, alone and frightened, unable to work, having to forage for food. He might become desperate and resort to crime. I thought it much better to keep him at Pemberley and train him to be my valet."

Darcy looked at Greenwood, that gentle giant, and he could not despise his father. Life was still life, and had meaning, no matter how it was engineered.

"Greenwood is not your real name, is it?" he asked.

Greenwood shook his head.

"What was your name?"

His father's creature took a pencil and wrote with large, childish letters: Igor Kuznetsov.

Darcy smiled. No wonder his father had renamed him. He said, "May I still call you Greenwood?"

Greenwood nodded.

"Very good. Now that I know who you are, what you are, I understand you and my father better. As far as I am concerned, you may live at Pemberley the rest of your life."

Greenwood smiled broadly and gave Darcy a hug that nearly crushed his ribs. The man might be slow moving, but he was strong.

"Thank you," Darcy gasped when he was released. "I do not need a valet, for I have my own, but you can be my Assistant."

Greenwood frowned and made a questioning noise.

"Yes, Assistant. I do not intend to follow in my father's footsteps entirely, but I would like to study medicine, beginning with my father's numerous notebooks."

He was humbled by what he had learned today. He had been given a glimpse of the secrets of heaven and earth. He did not know how much was the outward substance of things or the inner spirit of nature and the mysterious soul of man that intrigued him, but he knew that his inquiries would be directed to the metaphysical and the physical secrets of the world.

Darcy did not consider himself a genius like his father, but he believed that even a mind of moderate capacity which closely pursued one study must infallibly arrive at great proficiency in that study. Thus, into the depths of medical knowledge, he would dive with Greenwood, a modern Prometheus, by his side.

CHAPTER THREE

1811 – FIVE YEARS LATER

Longbourn was in a state of chaos as five young women and an anxious mother prepared for the Meryton Assembly. Lydia took Kitty's gloves without asking; Kitty lost one of her slippers and accused Lydia of hiding it. Mary, who like her father Mr. Bennet often withdrew from family conversation to read books, was found to be the culprit, for she had been sitting on it. With only one maid capable of arranging hair, each young woman was reduced to either sitting in her petticoats for an hour, waiting for her turn, or choosing to fend for herself. Elizabeth, the second oldest, helped Jane, the eldest, with her hair, but their mother found the resulting arrangement insufficiently elegant and ordered the maid to stop working on Kitty's tresses immediately and to tend to her oldest daughter.

"It's not fair!" Kitty protested as she stomped to her bedroom. "Why does Jane always go first?"

"Because she is the eldest," Mary, the middle daughter, said calmly.

"Because she is the prettiest," Mrs. Bennet said. "And the most likely to catch Mr. Bingley's attention."

Jane blushed. "Mama, we have not even met the man." Mr. Bingley was their new neighbour, a single young man rumoured to have a fortune of four thousand pounds a year. He had paid a morning visit to their father, but they had not seen him clearly from their upper window's view.

"No, but we will, and when we do, I want you to look your best. Hurry, child." Mrs. Bennet then looked at Elizabeth's hair with a critical eye. "You are fine. There is not much that can be done with your mop, anyway. No matter what we do, in ten minutes, it always looks untidy." Elizabeth was blessed - or cursed as her mother would say - with naturally curly hair that seemed to have a will of its own, often refusing to stay pinned up.

Mrs. Bennet reached over and removed the lace that had been tucked into the neckline of Elizabeth's high waisted gown. "There," she said happily, surveying her daughter's cleavage. "Now none of the gentlemen will be looking at your hair."

"Mama!" Elizabeth protested, but her mother did not listen.

Eventually they were all ready for the Assembly. Mr. Bennet chose to stay at home and enjoy a quiet household.

The Assembly was held in a public hall in Meryton, a town only a mile from Longbourn. The large room was decorated with garlands of pink muslin and lit with rows of standing candelabra. Mrs. Bennet quickly found her friend and neighbour Lady Lucas and the two women began critiquing the gowns of the other guests. "Can you believe it? Miss Cole is in her puce again. With her skin, that is not a happy choice."

Elizabeth whispered to her sister Jane. "How are you feeling?"

"I am fine. My scalp is still a little tender, though."

Their maid, when rushed, could be fierce with the hair pins. "Well, you look lovely," Elizabeth said. "Mr. Bingley, when he finally chooses to arrive, will be smitten instantly." Meryton gossip said that he would be attending the assembly with a party of guests from London. Elizabeth was looking forward to seeing some new faces.

Jane said quietly, "Please don't tease me. It is bad enough that Mama does so."

Elizabeth's conscience struck her. She enjoyed

finding the humour of their situation, but she never meant to be unkind. "Forgive me."

"No, I know you are only joking."

"It is difficult to be serious in a ballroom," Elizabeth added. "But I shall try." She found the entire situation ridiculous. All the unmarried women, looking their best, hoping to catch the eye and the admiration of an unmarried man.

At that point, both she and Jane were asked to dance by two of their male acquaintances, so they did so.

During the dance, Bingley and his party arrived. Elizabeth noticed them as she and her partner promenaded. There were three gentlemen and two ladies. She approved, for more gentlemen increased the probability of her dancing.

One gentleman, the tallest, had a commanding air.

But then she was forced to pay attention to the steps of her dance. She smiled at her partner and continued with the set.

Afterwards, she met her friend Charlotte Lucas at the refreshment table and sipped a glass of punch. "Have you met him?" she asked.

From her arch expression, Charlotte knew whom she was referencing. "Yes, and we will be dancing the next dance."

"Congratulations," Elizabeth murmured. She knew her mother would be vexed that Charlotte had the first opportunity to secure their new neighbour's affections.

"Here he comes," Charlotte whispered.

Mr. Bingley approached. He was a good looking man of medium height with an engaging smile. Nice hair, nice teeth, Elizabeth thought, which was always good. The last young man of fortune to ride through Meryton had been balding and had rivalled Sir William Lucas for size. "Miss Lucas," he said pleasantly. "Would you do me the honour of introducing your friend?"

Charlotte introduced them. Bingley bowed. He said, "I believe I have already met your oldest sister."

No doubt her mother had arranged that within seconds of his arrival.

As he and Charlotte joined the dance, Elizabeth walked over to where Mary was sitting. "Who is who?" she asked.

Mary answered, "The man of average height is Mr. Bingley. The two women are his sisters, Miss Bingley and Mrs. Hurst. The shorter gentleman is Mr. Hurst."

"And the tall gentleman?" Elizabeth looked across the room and saw him staring at them. Or glaring. It was difficult to determine at this distance and by candlelight.

"He is Mr. Darcy."

Elizabeth brightened. "Mr. Frankenstein Darcy of Pemberley?" she asked, catching her breath with hope. Could he be alive?

"I don't know," Mary said. "But they say he has a large estate in Derbyshire and has ten thousand a year."

Elizabeth had always found it amusing the way a man's income could become common knowledge within five minutes of his entrance, but tonight she could only smile with joy and relief that the young man she had met so long ago might not be dead. If this man was Frankenstein Darcy, she wanted to meet him.

She had often thought of that day at Pemberley. In some ways she considered it the last day of her childhood. The sun might shine or the clouds might lower, but nothing could appear to her as it had done before. Before she had been happy and carefree, and afterwards she had known that life could be unpredictable and cruel.

She walked around the room to the other side of the hall where the gentleman in question was standing. He wore ivory breeches, a gold waistcoat and a green coat. His hair was thick and dark. He was taller than she remembered with handsome features and a noble mein. The scar on his neck, if he had such a scar, was hidden by a brilliant white neckcloth.

She approached him. "Mr. Darcy," she said pleasantly. "I believe we have met before. If you are Mr. Frankenstein Darcy of Pemberley, that is."

He stiffened at her words and surveyed her with cool disdain. "That is my name, but I do not recall yours, ma'am." It was clear that he thought her presumptuous to imply an acquaintance that did not exist.

If she were timid, his frosty tones and his forbidding disagreeable countenance would have reduced her to a quivering jelly. But she was made of sterner stuff. She raised her chin and smiled brilliantly. "Miss Elizabeth Bennet, sir."

He bowed slightly. "Pleased to make your acquaintance, ma'am," he said with minimal civility. "Now, if you will excuse me, I will join my party."

With that, he left and strode over to speak with Miss Bingley.

Elizabeth stood for a moment, dumbfounded. What an arrogant, unpleasant man. Insufferable.

Seven years before, he had been a charming young man. She had liked him and had grieved to think him dead. She supposed she should be grateful that he was still alive, but oh, what a disagreeable man he had become.

She smiled at the irony. No doubt she had changed

as well, but hopefully for the better.

Rather than dwelling on this negative experience, Elizabeth turned her attention to the dance floor. She saw that Mr. Bingley was dancing with Jane. Her mother would be pleased.

Later in the evening, Mr. Bingley danced with Jane again. At this point, Elizabeth was sitting by herself, without a dance partner. She did not mind for it gave her a few moments for reflection. She also happened to overhear a conversation between Mr. Bingley and Mr. Darcy. Mr. Bingley had left the dance for a few minutes to press his friend to join it.

"Come, Darcy. I must have you dance. I hate to see you standing about by yourself in this stupid manner."

Elizabeth hid a smile behind her fan.

Bingley continued. "You had much better dance."

"I certainly shall not," Darcy said coolly. Elizabeth was surprised that he used such a superior tone with his friend as well. "You know how I much I detest it, unless I am particularly acquainted with my partner. At such an assembly as this, it would be insupportable. Your sisters are engaged, and there is not another woman in the room, whom it would not be a punishment to me to stand up with."

Elizabeth almost choked. Heavens, had there ever been such a conceited man?

Bingley cried, "I would not be so fastidious as you are for a kingdom! Upon my honour, I never met with so many pleasant girls in my life as I have this evening; and there are several of them who are uncommonly pretty."

"You are dancing with the only handsome girl in the room," said Darcy, looking at Jane.

So he wasn't completely blind, Elizabeth thought. Jane was the most beautiful girl in the room and she was pleased to hear Bingley say the same.

Bingley then said, "But there is one of her sisters sitting down just behind you, who is very pretty, and I dare say, very agreeable. Do let me ask my partner to introduce you."

Oh no, Elizabeth thought and wished she had chosen another location to sit.

"Which do you mean?" Darcy asked, and turning around, he looked for a moment at Elizabeth, till catching her eye, he withdrew his own and coldly said, "There is no need. She already forced an introduction upon me."

Elizabeth felt a blush rise in her cheeks.

"She is tolerable, I suppose, if one disregards the lack of manners, but she is not handsome enough to tempt me. You had better return to your partner and enjoy her smiles, for you are wasting your time with me."

Mr. Bingley followed his advice. Mr. Darcy walked off, and Elizabeth remained seated, striving to master her uncordial feelings towards him.

Eventually the ridiculousness of the situation tickled her playful sense of humour. The man was absurd and she was absurd to take offense. Why should she care what he thought of her?

She then told the story with great spirit among her friends, although she did not share the part about her having met him before. She saved that for an evening conversation with Jane.

When Jane and Elizabeth were alone, Jane said, "It was so strange to see Mr. Darcy again. He has certainly grown up. I am not certain I would have recognized him."

"Nor I," Elizabeth agreed. His face was thinner with the angles of his cheekbones and jaw more pronounced. He looked harder, more cynical.

"He seems so grand now."

Elizabeth was not as generous as Jane. She would use other adjectives to describe him. He was above being pleased. He was the proudest, most disagreeable man in the world.

Jane said, "And to think of his slighting you. That was poorly done."

Elizabeth smiled. "Yes, it was, wasn't it?"

"But I doubt he meant for his comments to be overheard."

Elizabeth laughed. "Does that make it any better? No Jane, you can choose to forgive him, but I will not."

"Mr. Bingley likes him. Mr. Darcy is one of his closest friends."

"I think Mr. Bingley must be a very patient man," Elizabeth said dryly.

Jane sighed. "Mr. Bingley is just what a young man ought to be: sensible, good humoured, lively; and I never saw such happy manners – so much ease, with such perfect good breeding!"

Elizabeth looked at her closely, wondering. Jane tended to like everyone. She never saw a fault in anybody. All the world was good and agreeable in her eyes. But she had never praised a young man so quickly upon first acquaintance. And there was an excitement about her, a happy glow, that Elizabeth had never seen.

Elizabeth did not believe in love at first sight, but could there be such a thing as love at first dance?

* * *

After the Meryton Assembly, Bingley and his guests ate a light supper at Netherfield before retiring. Darcy, according to his custom, declined everything except a bowl of soup.

Miss Bingley was anxious to hear his impressions of the assembly. "Mr. Darcy, did you enjoy yourself this evening?"

"Not particularly."

Bingley said, "I swear I shall give up on you, Darcy. Sometimes I think you are determined to be disagreeable. I wonder if it is a direct result of your medical training. All that illness and disease has weakened your affections and destroyed your taste for the simple pleasures of life. You see everyone as bits of blood and bone rather than the miraculous creatures that we are."

Darcy was amused by Bingley's poetic turn of phrase. "Would you rather I lie?"

"No, but I don't understand why you did not enjoy yourself tonight. I have never met with pleasanter people or prettier girls in my life. Everyone was most kind and attentive. There was no formality, no stiffness, and within half an hour, I felt as if I were acquainted with everyone in the room."

Darcy smiled grimly. "In two months, tell me if you feel the same."

"You think I will become bored with country life?"

"Yes, I do." In some ways, Bingley was like a dog - enthusiastic for one toy until another was introduced. He had rented Netherfield on impulse, but in a few weeks, he would return to Town on impulse as well. He had even talked a month before about wanting to join an expedition to search for a passage to the North Pole. Complete foolishness, but fortunately that idea had only lasted a day or two. Bingley liked the dream of travel and adventure more than the actuality.

Bingley was a good man and Darcy appreciated his easiness, his openness and the ductility of his temper, which was so different from his own, but sometimes he felt as if Bingley were a child and he were a hundred years older.

Miss Bingley intervened. "But you, Mr. Darcy, are a man of learning. I don't think you would be happy to spend your days merely socializing, whether in Town or here in the country."

"No, you are right. I miss my books." In truth, he had come to Netherfield to consider his future. He had recently finished medical training in Edinburgh and had passed his examinations. Technically he could practise medicine as a physician, but Pemberley and Georgiana were waiting for him. There was so much he could do with his life, he needed to determine what he should do.

"How can you miss your books when you brought a trunk filled with them?" Bingley said. "Surely you cannot read fifty books at once."

"No, but I might want to refer to them."

Miss Bingley said, "I believe Pemberley has the most delightful library." She had visited Pemberley the year before and often sang its praises.

Darcy said, "It ought to be good. It has been the work of many generations."

"And then you have added so much to it yourself. You are always buying books."

"I cannot comprehend the neglect of a family library in such days as these."

"Neglect! I am sure you neglect nothing that can add to the beauties of that noble place."

Darcy did not comment, for he knew he had neglected his home, partly from the wish to avoid painful memories. There was too much at home to remind him of his father's weaknesses and Wickham. Vaguely he listened as Miss Bingley stopped flattering him and began to tease her brother, encouraging him to use Pemberley as his model for the home he would someday build.

Darcy thought about Pemberley and his obligations as Master. He knew he must return home and eventually he must marry. He was old enough and would need an heir. Over the past summer he had considered several of the debutants as possible candidates. Unfortunately, he had overheard the most promising young woman talking about him to one of her friends.

The friend said, "Mr. Darcy is handsome, but have you seen the scar on his neck?"

The young woman shuddered. "Yes. Some of it."

It was normally hidden by his cravat.

"Horrifying," the friend agreed. "But I suppose ten thousand pounds a year makes up for it."

The young woman laughed. "If I do marry him, I will make him wear a neckcloth to bed."

Darcy could not help but wonder how many other women felt the same.

As a young man he had learned quickly that the possessions most esteemed by his fellow creatures were: high and unsullied descent united with riches. Through a quirk of fate, he was blessed with both. A man might be respected with only one, like Bingley, but without either, a man was often considered dross.

Darcy inwardly railed against the injustice of society – was there no accommodation for talent and dedication?

He wished he were more like his father, able to accept each man as his equal, but it was not in his nature. He saw too clearly the vanity, pettiness and avarice of others.

Added to this was the curse of being a wealthy man

– having to view all social interactions with suspicion. Darcy had few true friends, and those he had, like Bingley, were valued highly.

Eventually the conversation returned to that evening's assembly. Bingley said he thought Miss Bennet was as beautiful as an angel.

Darcy thought his admiration excessive. He countered Bingley's praise with the observation that she smiled too much.

"Perhaps she does," Miss Bingley said. "But I still like her. I think she is a sweet girl, and I would not object to knowing her better."

"Then you will call on her," Bingley said hopefully.

"Yes, to be sure."

Oh Bingley, Darcy thought as Bingley smiled happily. *Do not fall in love again. It will not last.*

CHAPTER FOUR

Over the next few weeks, the ladies of Longbourn waited on those of Netherfield and the visit was returned in due form. The families also met at various homes in the neighbourhood for dinners and card parties. Darcy was concerned to see how often Bingley spoke with Jane Bennet. She was a pretty, well-behaved girl, but her family was atrocious. Mrs. Bennet was loud and vulgar, Mr. Bennet vague and ineffectual, the younger Bennet girls silly and giggly. And then there was Elizabeth Bennet. Darcy had not quite made up his mind about her.

He did not speak with her himself, because he did not want to encourage her, but he watched her converse with others. He noticed that her face, which was average at best, was rendered uncommonly intelligent by the beautiful expression of her dark eyes.

And her figure that he had dismissed as lacking

perfect symmetry, was upon second and third consideration, light and pleasing.

Her manners, although not those of the fashionable world, were playful and charming.

He was fascinated and wanted to know more of her.

One evening they were both at the home of Sir William Lucas, a good natured but simple man who often spoke of his reception at St. James. Darcy attended to Elizabeth's conversations, overhearing her speak to different guests. He thought he had been discreet in his eavesdropping, until she confronted him. "Do you not think, Mr. Darcy, that I expressed myself uncommonly well just now, when I was teasing Colonel Forster to give us a ball at Meryton?"

He refused to be embarrassed. Anyone could listen to conversations at a party. It was not a crime. "Yes, you spoke with great energy, but dancing is a subject which always makes a lady energetic."

"You are severe on us."

She was joking, but there was an element of truth in her tone. Darcy considered what he would say in response, but then he was saved by the interruption of Charlotte Lucas who asked her to play on the pianoforte.

Elizabeth protested that she was not prepared to play before people who were in the habit of hearing the very best performers. Did she refer to himself, he wondered. Then one of her younger sisters said, "Oh, Lizzy, please play."

Lizzy. The name seemed to jog a memory.

Elizabeth agreed and walked over to the instrument. She sat down, chose a song from a stack of music sheets and began to play. Her performance was pleasing, although by no means capital. But he found himself distracted, unable to give the music his full attention.

Her sister had called her Lizzy.

Could she be the Lizzy who had helped him the day he was shot? He did not remember the girl well, other than her skipping that rock and her unflappable attitude. She had been skinny with wild curly hair.

But that was seven years ago; she would have been a child then and a young woman now. Naturally she would have changed physically, but there was something similar in her tone of voice and the way she challenged him.

He began to think Elizabeth Bennet must be the girl. She had said they had met before and he had snubbed her, thinking she was like the myriad women who had fawned over him since his father's death.

That had been unjust of him. He decided to speak to her and had to wait until she finished playing. After two songs, her sister Mary eagerly took her place at the pianoforte. Mary had neither genius nor taste. Technically she played better than her older sister, but she had a pedantic air and conceited manner which lessened the listeners' pleasure. And worse for Darcy, she played some Scotch and Irish airs which encouraged the younger Bennets and some of the officers to join in dancing at one end of the room.

Darcy was frustrated. With all this noise, he would not be able to talk to Elizabeth without shouting.

Sir William approached him. "What a charming amusement for young people this is, Mr. Darcy," he said. "There is nothing like dancing after all. I consider it as one of the first refinements of polished societies."

Darcy strove to hide his irritation. He said stiffly, "And of all the less polished societies as well. Every savage can dance." He frowned as he saw Bingley take Jane to join in the dancing. Did he not see that by singling her out he might give rise to expectations? If he wasn't careful, these provincials would snap him up and he would be caught like a fish on a hook.

Sir William saw Elizabeth walk by and said, "My dear Miss Eliza, why are you not dancing? Mr. Darcy, you must allow me to present this young lady to you as a very desirable dance partner. Surely you cannot refuse to dance, I am sure, when so much beauty is before you."

Elizabeth blushed, embarrassed by her neighbour's excessive praise.

At that moment, Darcy realized that he would like to dance with her, but Elizabeth drew back.

"Indeed, Sir, I have not the least intention of dancing. I entreat you not to suppose that I moved this way in order to beg for a partner."

Darcy said, "It would be my honour."

She shook her head. "No, thank you. I already know you dislike the amusement and I would not want to tempt you with my handsomeness –" she waited until Sir. William was out of earshot to add quietly, "or the lack thereof."

So she had heard him at the Meryton Assembly. Darcy said quickly, "That was unkind of me. I should not have said it."

"No, sir. You should not have."

"Especially when I consider that you may have saved my life."

Elizabeth's eyes narrowed. "Are you saying that a woman must save your life before you condescend to be civil to her?"

"That was not my meaning."

"I don't care to understand your meaning, sir. I am glad you are not dead, but that does not mean I wish to speak with you further." She looked at him with an arch smile and turned away.

He stood for a moment, watching her, thinking over their conversation, when Miss Bingley accosted him. "I can guess the subject of your reverie."

"I should imagine not." He noted how Elizabeth had worn a simple, pleasant gown with minimal lace and a single gold chain about her graceful throat. In contrast, Miss Bingley's gown was heavy with expensive trim and her jewellery thick and gaudy. Miss Bingley's hair, instead of sweet, natural curls, was ornate and stiff, topped with a headdress, complete with two plumes that bobbed and swayed as she spoke. He was briefly reminded of cultures in India where young women wore their dowry. In some ways, it was not that different in England today.

Miss Bingley said, "You are considering how insupportable it would be to pass many evenings in this manner – in such society. The insipidity and yet the noise of these people. Their nothingness and yet their self-importance. Am I not correct?"

"Your conjecture is totally wrong, I assure you," he said calmly. "My mind was engaged elsewhere. I have been meditating on the war between men and women and how a pair of fine eyes in the face of a pretty woman can bestow pleasure and pain."

Miss Bingley asked, "And which young lady has

inspired your reflections?"

"Miss Elizabeth Bennet."

As soon as Darcy answered, he knew that had been an error in judgment. Miss Bingley would tease him now.

"Miss Elizabeth Bennet!" Miss Bingley exclaimed, her voice rising shrilly. "I am all astonishment. Does she give you pain, sir? She is reputed to be a wit, but I have found her to be overly caustic."

He saw Elizabeth glance at them with distaste and then turn away.

"Let us talk of something else," he said in a quiet tone. "Would you like to dance?"

Miss Bingley readily agreed, although she did complain that the music was inferior and the dancing area too small.

As he moved through the steps of the dance, he watched Elizabeth who stood to one side of the room, speaking to her friend Charlotte. She seemed surprised to see him dancing and watched him coolly, her face expressionless.

He felt that Elizabeth Bennet was like a lightning bolt to his heart. It was uncertain whether she would enliven him or kill him outright, but the wisest course of action would be to fashion an emotional lightning rod.

* * *

Jane received a letter from Caroline Bingley, inviting her to dine at Netherfield. She mentioned the matter at the breakfast table. "Ooh, Jane," Mrs. Bennet said happily. "I am certain Mr. Bingley had something to do with the invitation, but it would be too much for him to ask you personally. At least not until you are engaged."

"No, Mama," Jane protested. "You presume too much. The invitation is from Miss Bingley only. In it, she states that the gentlemen will be dining with the officers."

Mrs. Bennet said, "That is disappointing, to be sure, but let us see if we can improve upon it."

Jane frowned. "I do not understand."

Her mother said, "You don't want to go all the way there and not see Mr. Bingley, do you?"

"That is the invitation, yes."

"Silly girl. We must contrive a way for you to spend the night."

"Mama!" Jane was scandalized.

Lydia giggled.

"I know," Mrs. Bennet said simply. "You must ride a horse rather than take the carriage. It looks like rain and you will be forced to spend the night."

Elizabeth said, "Surely you are joking, Mama."

"I never joke about matrimony."

Jane glanced at her father for moral support, but he merely shrugged and glanced at his newspaper.

"What shall I do?" Jane asked later, when she and Elizabeth were alone. "I do not want to impose upon the Bingleys."

"Then pray it does not rain," Elizabeth said bluntly. "And take an umbrella."

In the end, however, it did rain and Jane did not return to Longbourn in the evening. Mrs. Bennet was very pleased with herself and smiled throughout dinner.

In the morning, they received a note from Jane saying that she had caught a cold and that her hostesses had invited her to remain until she felt better. She assured them that she was fine except for a sore-throat and headache.

Mrs. Bennet was smug. "See, Lizzy?" she said. "What do you think of my plans now? I told you how it would be. Ah, Mr. Bingley. He is such a kind, well-mannered gentleman."

"And he has such a nice large house," Mary added.

"But no red coat," Lydia said. She and Kitty giggled. The militia was currently stationed at Meryton and the two youngest Bennet daughters thought soldiers were the epitome of romance.

Mr. Bennet said coolly, "My dear Mrs. Bennet, if Jane should have a dangerous fit of illness, if she should die, it will be a comfort for you to know that it was all in pursuit of Mr. Bingley, with or without a red coat." He opened his newspaper with a snap of annoyance that silenced his daughters.

"Oh, I am not afraid of her dying. People do not die of little trifling colds," Mrs. Bennet said, justifying herself. "She will be taken good care of. As long as she stays there, it is all very well."

Elizabeth was not so sanguine. The rain the night before had been torrential and she worried that Jane was minimizing her ailments. She asked her father if she could take the carriage, but it was not available. Elizabeth was no horsewoman, so she determined to walk to Netherfield.

"What nonsense is this, Lizzy," her mother said. "Three miles in all that dirt? You will not be fit to be seen when you get there."

"Do you wish me to send for the horses?" her father asked. "I suppose I can make arrangements."

"No, indeed. I do not mind the walk. It is only three miles and the fresh air will do me good. I shall be back by dinner."

Kitty and Lydia walked with her as far as Meryton for they planned to call on one of the officers' wives, and Elizabeth walked the rest of the way to Netherfield by herself. She crossed field after field at a quick pace, jumping over stiles and springing over puddles with impatient activity. She passed her favourite rock skipping location without stopping. She was anxious to see Jane.

As she neared Netherfield, she walked up through landscaped gardens. There was a stone fountain, surrounded by four marble statues – half dressed women representing the different seasons. As she walked past the statue of Autumn, a bare breasted, stocky woman holding a basket of fruit, she was startled by a large man stepping out from behind another statue.

He was huge with broad shoulders and a massive chest. His arms hung awkwardly and his face was horribly scarred.

In her surprise, her boots slipped on the wet grass and she lost her balance. Elizabeth cried out as she fell backward. Her head struck stone, she felt a moment of pain, and then everything was blissfully dark.

CHAPTER FIVE

Darcy sat at the breakfast table with Bingley and listened to his sisters discuss Jane Bennet. "She has a cold," Miss Bingley was saying. "I don't think it particularly bad, but perhaps we should call Mr. Jones, just to be certain."

"I can look at her," Darcy offered.

Miss Bingley blinked and then gave a little laugh. "Oh, yes. I don't know why I did not think of it sooner. You are a doctor, after all. I suppose I tend to think of you as Master of Pemberley."

"Can I not be both?" he asked.

Bingley asked, "Would you feel comfortable examining an acquaintance? Would that not feel strange?"

Darcy said stiffly, "If you think Miss Bennet would not like it, you may send for Mr. Jones."

"No," Bingley said quickly. "I did not mean to give

offense. I am sure you are an excellent physician, I just thought –"

"I am a doctor," Darcy said. "I can set aside my personal feelings when it comes to caring for a patient."

"Then by all means," Bingley said. "Perhaps after breakfast, you can –"

None of them heard Bingley finish, for at that moment, the doors of the breakfast room opened and Greenwood staggered into the room, carrying Elizabeth Bennet in his arms.

They made an alarming picture of contrasts: the huge, scarred man carrying the beautiful young maiden. His skin grey with a yellow overcast, hers deathly pale. She was unconscious, one arm hanging limply, her skirt a cascade of white. Her dark curly hair, free from a bonnet, flowed over his arm.

Mrs. Hurst shrieked and fainted, collapsing onto the table.

Darcy rose to his feet. "Elizabeth!"

Miss Bingley cried out, "What have you done to her?"

Greenwood stepped back, momentarily confused.

"He has done nothing!" Darcy said sharply and hurried to the large man's side. "Set her down on a couch." He pointed to a nearby sitting room and then followed Greenwood and Elizabeth. In just a moment, she was lying down. Greenwood stood several feet away, his hands clutched in front of himself, his eyes concerned.

Darcy knelt by Elizabeth's side. He checked her breathing and placed his ear on her chest. Her heartbeat was steady, thank goodness. "What happened?" he demanded.

Greenwood made hand motions of a person walking and then falling.

"She slipped?"

Greenwood nodded.

Darcy gently examined her head and felt a large bump behind one ear. There was a little blood, but not much.

"Will she be all right?" Bingley asked.

"I do not know, yet," Darcy said. "She has struck her head and appears concussed. There may be internal swelling." He opened her eyes and looked closely at them. Her pupils were dilated, but fortunately not of different sizes.

"What can I do?" Miss Bingley asked.

Leave me alone, Darcy thought, but instead he said, "Get me some cold wet cloths."

A footman was sent to the kitchens.

"I must also check for further injury or broken bones," Darcy announced as he gently touched her arms and legs.

Miss Bingley gasped, but fortunately remained silent during his examination. Not for the first time, Darcy regretted the social customs that required him to examine young women fully dressed. It would be simpler to check for bruises and scrapes if he was able to loosen her clothes as he could if she were a man.

"It appears that her head injury is the extent of her trouble," he said finally. With one damp cloth, he gently wiped her face and her hands. With a second, he gingerly touched the back of her head.

Miss Bennet let her breath out in a hiss and flinched with pain. Her beautiful eyes opened.

Thank God, Darcy prayed.

"Mr. Darcy?" she said in confusion. "My head hurts."

She tried to sit up, but he pressed on her shoulder to keep her horizontal. "Shh, Miss Bennet," he said calmly. "You have fallen and hit your head. You need rest. Lie still."

"Where am I?"

"At Netherfield."

She was confused. "I don't remember. Did I come to see Jane?"

That would explain her presence. "I think so," Darcy said. "But now you will be a patient as well." He turned to Bingley and his sister. "She is going to need to lie down for at least a day or two, possibly more. Can you put her up in a room next to her sister?"

"Yes, of course," Bingley said. "Whatever she needs."

But Miss Bingley who was beginning to be alarmed by an invasion of Bennets, said, "Wouldn't she be better at Longbourn with her own family?"

"No," Darcy said firmly. "I must keep her under observation for two days and she should not be moved. Even simple head injuries can be fatal."

Elizabeth frowned. "Are you a doctor, Mr. Darcy?"

"Yes."

She closed her eyes wearily. "You have an appalling bedside manner. Go away."

* * *

After Elizabeth was settled in her own room, Darcy visited Jane Bennet's room as well. She was more tidy than her sister. A lady's maid had fashioned her hair and she was wearing a neat robe fashioned like a pelisse. She sat up in her bed. "I don't think I am very ill, Mr. Darcy," she said, then coughed, a quiet, delicate cough.

"I am glad to hear it," Darcy said matter-of-factly. "And I hope you are right." He paused. "Are you willing to have me examine you, or would you rather wait for Mr. Jones? I have already sent for him so I can obtain any medicines I may need."

Jane glanced nervously at the young woman servant who had accompanied Darcy into the room. "You may examine me," she said. "I did not know until today that you are a doctor."

"No, it is not common knowledge for I have not begun my practise."

A moment of concern crossed her face.

"But I do know what I am doing, Miss Bennet," he assured her. "Shall we begin?"

She nodded.

He touched her forehead and felt that she had a slight fever. He looked at her eyes and asked her to stick out her tongue. It was slightly swollen. "Open your mouth," he said. He was pleased to see that although her throat was red, there were no white patches. He touched her neck and the glands below her jaw and chin. She flinched.

"Tender?" he asked.

"Yes."

"Are you having difficulty swallowing?"

"A little."

"Now I will listen to your breathing." He saw her eyes widen and he took from his medical case a wooden tube designed specifically for this purpose, to be able to hear his patients and still preserve their modesty. He placed the tube with one end over the upper part of her left breast. He leaned forward and put his right ear to the other end of the tube.

He was silent for a minute, listening to her breathing. She had a little congestion, but it was not alarming.

"You are correct, Miss Bennet," he said finally. "You have a little cold and I do not believe it is serious."

"Thank you. Will I need bloodletting?'

"No."

"Mr. Jones often recommends bloodletting and I don't mind if it is necessary," Jane said bravely.

Darcy clenched his teeth to keep from commenting on Mr. Jones's medical skills. "Bloodletting is rarely necessary," he said finally. "I find it often makes a patient weak. I prefer tonics, such as vinegar water."

Jane nodded.

Darcy smiled. Vinegar had many medical uses and had the added benefit of tasting unpleasant, which made patients feel that they were consuming something efficacious. "I will prepare a tonic. Also, for the next few days, I want you to eat simply. No heavy sauces or spices. Simple meat and vegetables only. Boiled eggs. And bone broth. I don't want you to tax your digestion."

"Yes, sir."

Darcy closed his medical case.

"I heard that Elizabeth is here as well. How is she doing?"

"She slipped and hit her head, but was awake and is sleeping now."

"May I see her?" Jane asked.

"Not yet. I would prefer you to be better first."

"Very well, thank you, Dr. Darcy."

After Darcy left her room, he also checked on Elizabeth Bennet, who was sleeping. She was so beautiful and pale as she lay on the bed. His heart felt like a drum beating in his chest when he thought of what had happened, what might still happen. The maid sitting on a chair beside her bed asked, "Do you need anything, sir?"

"No." He stood for several minutes, watching her breathe, then left the room. He turned down a hall to return to the sitting room and found Greenwood standing in the hall, waiting patiently for him.

"Thank you for your help this morning," Darcy said.

Greenwood made a questioning noise and made a motion indicating a curvaceous female figure.

Darcy assumed he meant Elizabeth. "Miss Elizabeth is doing better. She is resting."

Greenwood then lifted his chin and looked down his nose in a conceited manner and wiggled his fingers under one ear to indicate dangly earrings.

Darcy nodded, recognizing his sign. "Yes. I noticed that. I hope Miss Bingley's comments did not upset you. She isn't very intelligent at times."

Greenwood gave a harsh bark, his form of laughter.

"Just try not to surprise our hostess for a few days," Darcy suggested.

* * *

Elizabeth could not believe how horrible she felt, just from a bump on the head. She was embarrassed that she had slipped and fallen. She felt foolish because she had meant to care for Jane and had ended up needing even more care herself. She had vomited twice, was dizzy when she tried to walk, and sometimes had a ringing in her ears.

When she woke the first day, that evening, she saw a vase full of flowers beside her bed. "How lovely."

"They're from the monster," the servant girl said.

"The monster?"

"Mr. Greenwood," the girl corrected. "Mr. Bingley says we're not supposed to call him a monster, but he hardly looks like a man, does he?"

Elizabeth thought of the man who had startled her.

She supposed it was Darcy's father's valet, the man Mrs. Reynolds had mentioned years before. He was frighteningly ugly with large deep scars on his face and one shoulder slightly higher than the other. "He brought me flowers?"

"Yes, he really is a sweetheart. He spends a lot of time in the garden. He likes flowers."

Elizabeth smiled. "Well, if you see him, thank him for me."

"I will, miss."

On her second day there, her mother and sisters came to visit. "Oh my poor dear girl," Mrs. Bennet exclaimed, patting her hand, then turned her attention towards Mr. Bingley and his friend. "She is much too ill to be moved, isn't she Mr. Darcy?"

Darcy nodded. "I don't think she should leave until she is completely recovered."

"And how long will that be?"

"At least several more days," Darcy said.

Mrs. Bennet nodded happily. "Whatever is best for my daughter."

Miss Bingley said, "You may depend upon it, Madam, that your daughters shall receive every possible attention while they remain with us."

"You are so good," Mrs. Bennet said. "I am sure, if it was not for such good friends, I do not know what would become of them. Poor Elizabeth. And Jane, too. She has been ill in her own right, although not as bad as her sister. It is almost as if you have set up your own hospital," she said as a little joke, but then continued. "Mr. Bingley, I am certain you have noticed what an excellent patient Jane has been. She has the sweetest temper I have ever met with. I often tell my other girls they are nothing to her."

Elizabeth noticed that her mother had no praise for her, but thankfully that was because it had never occurred to her that Mr. Darcy might be a matrimonial prospect. Mrs. Bennet did not like Mr. Darcy and considered him a most disagreeable man.

Mrs. Bennet looked around the sitting room with pleasure. "You have a sweet room here, Mr. Bingley, and a charming prospect over that gravel walk. I don't know a place in the country that is equal to Netherfield. You will not think of quitting it in a hurry, I hope."

At least not until you have married my daughter, Elizabeth mentally added.

Her mother continued, praising Jane and Bingley.

Lydia spoke up, asking Mr. Bingley how soon he would host the ball he had promised.

Elizabeth groaned and closed her eyes, embarrassed by her obnoxious family.

"Are you in pain, Miss Elizabeth?" Mr. Darcy asked quietly.

"No, merely tired," she lied.

Eventually Bingley promised to hold a ball as soon as she and Jane recovered. Darcy said, "Are there enough people in Meryton to warrant a ball?"

"Certainly there are," Mrs. Bennet interjected, visibly annoyed by Mr. Darcy. "There are few neighbourhoods larger. We dine with four and twenty families."

Miss Bingley smirked. "If necessary, we will invite our acquaintances from London."

"It seems an inconvenience," Darcy commented.

"Don't try to dissuade me," Bingley teased. "For I am determined. You need not attend, if you do not wish." He turned to Jane, "Darcy dislikes dancing."

"How strange," Mrs. Bennet said. "I don't believe I have ever met a true gentleman who did not like dancing." She had heard about Darcy's refusing to dance with Elizabeth at the Assembly and she considered it a personal affront. If she were a man, she might have challenged him to a duel.

"Mama," Elizabeth interjected. "Surely you acknowledge that everyone can have their own preferences."

"Yes, but it is a sign of good breeding to accept and

enjoy the efforts of one's host. Indeed, I believe Sir William would agree that it is almost a duty for young men to dance. Those who choose to neglect that duty, fancying themselves above it, quite mistake the matter."

There was an awkward silence after this comment, but Mrs. Bennet did not seem to notice. She continued, "Although Jane will recover in a day or so, I think she should stay, to help with Elizabeth, don't you agree, Mr. Bingley?"

Bingley looked at Jane and smiled. "Yes, certainly. I would not want to separate your daughters, ma'am."

Darcy stifled a rude noise, that might have been a mocking laugh. He turned it into a cough.

"Oh, no, Mr. Darcy, I hope you are not coming down with a cold as well," Miss Bingley said with alarm.

He cleared his throat. "I am fine. I am rarely ill," he assured her and walked away from the conversation to stand by a window and look outside.

"Darcy prides himself on his health," Mr. Bingley said. "And in all the years I have known him, I don't think I have seen him ill more than twice."

"You must have a strong constitution," Elizabeth said, wanting to make up for her mother's rudeness.

He glanced at her. "I believe in prevention. A

sensible diet, adequate rest and regular bathing can do much to prolong life."

Bingley said, "What is it you are always saying – that cleanliness is next to godliness?"

"My father thought that cleanliness was a form of godliness. Dirt is the harbinger of disease and death."

"Was your father a doctor as well?" Elizabeth asked.

"Of a sort. He was an amateur but a remarkable scientist. He had many interests, primarily chemistry and natural philosophy."

Mrs. Bennet, bored by the turn the conversation was taking, said, "Sometimes parents can keep children too clean and not let them enjoy the world. Lizzy, for example, loved to play in the dirt. Even Jane, although she has outgrown that. A little dirt never hurt anyone, I have always thought."

Elizabeth longed to speak, but could think of nothing useful to say.

Miss Bingley laughed scornfully. "I hope we will not need to check everyone's hands before the ball."

Mrs. Bennet laughed as well, mistakenly thinking that she had found an ally in Miss Bingley. After a few more minutes of stilted conversation, Mrs. Bennet ordered the carriage and left, happy that she had managed to get two daughters living at Netherfield, even if it was only for a few days.

CHAPTER SIX

Darcy insisted that both the Misses Bennet stay in their rooms for the remainder of the day and eat dinner in their rooms. "Tomorrow, you may both get up and move about. Miss Elizabeth may even benefit from a short walk out of doors, if she takes someone's arm."

"Do you think I may still be dizzy, Mr. Darcy?"

"I want you to be careful," he said.

"Yes, doctor," she said politely, but he saw the mutinous look she gave her sister.

Darcy left the room quickly, alarmed by the thought that if she did take a walk, he wanted her to be with him, holding his arm.

This would never do.

He steeled himself, reminding himself of the inferiority of her connections. Of her insufferable mother.

But she fascinated him. He wanted to talk to her to

hear what she would say next.

The next day, he managed to avoid her for most of the day until evening when they all met in the drawing room. Several of them were at the loo table, but Darcy had decided to write to his sister instead. He noticed that Elizabeth had also decided to read rather than play cards, to Mr. Hurst's amusement. He called her "singular" for preferring books.

Miss Bingley pestered Darcy for a few minutes, asking him to mention her good wishes to his sister. She asked, "Is Miss Darcy much grown since the spring? Will she be as tall as I am?"

Darcy said, "I think she will. She is now about Miss Elizabeth Bennet's height or a little taller."

Miss Bingley said, "How I long to see her again! I never met with anybody who delighted me so much. Such a countenance, such manners! And so extremely accomplished for her age! Her performance on the piano-forte is exquisite."

Darcy saw Elizabeth look down to hide her amusement at Miss Bingley's raptures. Darcy often found Miss Bingley irritating, but since she was the sister of his best friend, he had learned to ignore her.

Bingley said, "It is amazing to me how young ladies have the patience to be so very accomplished. They all paint tables, cover screens and net purses. I am sure I never heard a young lady spoken of for the first time, without being informed that she was very accomplished." He smiled at Jane as he spoke.

"If everyone is accomplished, then it loses its value as a compliment," Darcy commented. "I believe the label is used too frequently. I believe I know no more than half a dozen young women who truly deserve the designation."

"Oh, I agree," Miss Bingley said. "Too many women claim to be accomplished but are not."

Elizabeth said, "You must comprehend a great deal in your idea of an accomplished woman."

"Yes, I do." Darcy said.

"Oh certainly," Miss Bingley said and elaborated further. "An accomplished woman must surpass what is usually met with. She should have a thorough knowledge of music, singing, drawing, dancing and the modern languages, to deserve the word. And besides all this, she must possess a certain something in her air and manner of walking, the tone of her voice, her address and expressions that shows her superiority."

Darcy glanced at Elizabeth and said, "And to all this, she must add something more substantial, the improvement of her mind by extensive reading."

Elizabeth snapped the book she was reading shut as

if annoyed by his subtle compliment. "I am no longer surprised at your knowing only six accomplished women. I rather wonder now at your knowing any."

"Are you so severe upon your sex as to doubt the possibility?"

"I never saw such a woman."

Mrs. Hurst and Miss Bingley protested that they knew many such women in Town. Mr. Hurst complained about their inattention and they returned to the card table.

Mr. Darcy finished his letter. As he folded it, he saw that Elizabeth was watching him as if curious.

"Miss Bennet?" he asked.

"Yes?"

"You appear to be puzzled. Is there something you wish to ask me?"

"Only this. You are a man of science. Rather than being content to manage your estate, you have spent years acquiring medical knowledge. Why?"

No one had been bold enough to ask him outright before. "I find anatomy fascinating and I wish to be of some good in the world."

"So you seek a noble purpose."

He frowned. "To some degree, yes. Don't we all?"

"But not women, given your definition of accomplishments. Do you think half of the human race should limit themselves?"

"Are you negating the social benefits of grace and beauty? The arts can provide joy, and many women seem to have a talent for it."

She said, "A talent because it is expected, or a talent because it is freely chosen? How would you feel if your worth was measured by your beauty or your ability to sing?"

Darcy smiled. She had obviously never heard him sing. "Are you one of those women who want to study architecture or politics?"

"Not particularly, but I am not talking about myself. I am thinking about society as a whole."

"Then you are a philosopher."

"In a way. I like to observe people and determine their characters. I want to understand them."

"And now I am under your microscopic lens."

"Yes, for you are before me. I have already taken the measure of Mr. Bingley and his sisters. You are more complex."

He bowed his head. "I am glad to give you some occupation while you are convalescing."

Miss Bingley, noticing the seriousness of their conversation, interrupted, announcing that she would play music and asked Elizabeth to turn the pages for her. Elizabeth agreed, and Darcy watched her as she walked over to the instrument.

This was madness, he thought as he admired the sway of her walk. He must find something else to think on.

* * *

Elizabeth watched with interest as Bingley attended to Jane, making certain she was sitting near the fire and protected from the draft. When Elizabeth walked by, she overheard them talking about the benefits of travel.

Bingley was explaining that he could not remain happy in one place for long. "It is the lure of the unknown, Miss Bennet, that spurs me onward. I think I have a high need for novelty."

"Where would you like to travel?" Jane asked.

"I would love to do the Grand Tour, but Napoleon is not very accommodating at present."

Elizabeth smiled. "Neither are the Colonies."

"No," Bingley said. "I may have to settle for going north."

Jane said, "To Scotland?"

"More north. To the North Pole."

"Good heavens, Charles, are you talking about that again?" Miss Bingley said, also walking past. "Don't encourage him, Miss Bennet, or he will abandon us all in his wild scheme."

"There are those," Darcy said, "who champion any change, just because it is new and they are bored."

"Are you never bored, Mr. Darcy?" Elizabeth asked pointedly.

He seemed to take her question seriously. "I am, but that, no doubt, is a failure on my part. As I apply myself to my studies, I should have ample facts or questions to occupy my mind no matter my physical situation."

"By study, do you refer to medicine?"

"All science," he said. "In scientific pursuit there is continual food for discovery and wonder."

"I know little of science," she admitted.

"Then you do not know enough. At some point, the pursuit of knowledge becomes addicting. None but those who have experienced them can conceive of the enticements of science."

"Perhaps I do not wish to become an addict," Elizabeth countered.

* * *

Elizabeth was feeling better. She walked outside with Jane and she spent time playing the pianoforte. One day as she practised, she glanced up and saw Greenwood in the doorway.

When he recognized her, he shrank back into the hallway.

She paused her hands on the keys. "No, do not go," she said. "You may listen if you wish. I do not mind, as long as you do not mind a few errors."

She motioned for him. "Come in, sit down."

Greenwood hesitated, then obeyed. He chose a chair across the room from her and sat down awkwardly.

She asked him if he wished to sit closer, but he shook his head.

She played a piece by Handel, a haunting, peaceful melody. When she looked up again, she saw that Greenwood had closed his eyes and had a calm, euphoric look on his scarred face.

Elizabeth was glad that she could give him a little joy. When he opened his eyes, she said, "Thank you for helping me when I fell. I am in your debt."

He made a noise and shook his head, as if denying that.

She continued, "Is there any song you would like to hear? Do you know music? Can you read it?"

She held out several music sheets for his perusal. He walked closer, took the papers and glanced at them for a few minutes, then chose one.

"Ah, Herr Beethoven," she said. "Good choice, although we will see if my fingers are up to the challenge."

When she said the word fingers, her voice quivered, for she remembered his large, thick fingers and she looked away nervously. She took a deep breath to steady herself and began to play. Greenwood sat down again, this time closer to her.

She was nearing the end of the piece, when Miss Bingley entered the room. "Ah, Miss Eliza," she said. "I could tell it wasn't Louisa playing for she has more skill, but I am glad to see that you are recovering."

Elizabeth silenced her hands. "Yes, I am feeling better."

Miss Bingley frowned at Greenwood. "Don't you have something better to do? Some task for Mr. Darcy?"

Greenwood bowed and left the room.

Miss Bingley waited until he was gone to say, "I don't know why Darcy keeps him on. His face is so hideous; it turns my stomach."

"Perhaps he sees the man inside."

Miss Bingley shuddered. "If I were ever Mistress of Pemberley," she said, then caught herself. She smiled. "Miss Eliza, I was looking for your sister Miss Bennet."

"I believe she is upstairs in her room, resting."

"Very good, thank you."

That afternoon Elizabeth spoke to Jane and made plans to return to Longbourn. They wrote to their mother, requesting the carriage, which she denied. Jane then spoke to Miss Bingley about borrowing Mr. Bingley's carriage.

Mr. Bingley was concerned about their health; he conferred with Darcy, and the decision was made for them to leave on Sunday, after morning service.

Elizabeth did not see Darcy much at all, he scarcely spoke ten words to her through the whole of Saturday. At one time they were left by themselves for half an hour and he adhered most conscientiously to his book and would not even look at her.

Elizabeth decided that although he had talent as a doctor, his social skills were woefully inadequate. The sooner she and Jane could leave Netherfield, the better.

* * *

Elizabeth and Jane returned to Longbourn on Sunday. Mrs. Bennet wished they had stayed longer, but she was pleased that at least Bingley had been able to see Jane with her health restored for several days. "Not that he could not have fallen in love with you when your nose was pink, but it is good that he saw you looking better."

Mr. Bennet asked Elizabeth about her injury. "Has your brain recovered?"

"I believe so," she answered. "I am still a little tired,

but Mr. Darcy assures me that I will have no lasting harm."

Mr. Bennet smiled. "Strange to think of him as a doctor."

"Yes," she agreed. "But he appears competent."

"Good. I am glad you have returned. The conversations in this house have been reduced to idiocy without you and Jane."

The next morning at breakfast, Mr. Bennet announced that his cousin Mr. Collins would be arriving that evening.

"Mr. Collins!" Mrs. Bennet exclaimed. "I cannot abide that name."

"Should he go by another?" Mr. Bennet asked calmly.

She glared at him. "Do not tease me, Mr. Bennet. You know exactly how I feel."

"I do," he said. "For you have been telling me these past twenty years."

"I don't understand how a man's property can be taken from his own wife and children. It is not fair, Mr. Bennet."

"It is the terms of the entail. There is nothing I can do about it."

Elizabeth glanced at Jane. They had heard their mother wax eloquent on the subject for years as well.

Since their father had no male heir, upon his death his property would pass to his cousin, Mr. Collins. Mrs. Bennet would be left with the settlements made at her marriage. That was why she was so anxious for her daughters to marry well. If they did not marry men with money, their family could be destitute.

"I thought you and Mr. Collins were estranged," Elizabeth said to her father.

"His father and I had a falling out, yes, but now the son is extending an olive branch." He glanced at his letter. "He apologizes for being the means of injuring our daughters and says he is willing to make them every possible amends."

Mrs. Bennet brightened. "Every possible amends?"

Kitty said, "What can that mean?"

"He might want to marry one of us," Mary said.

Lydia laughed. "Do you think he has a red coat?"

"I hope he's handsome," Kitty said.

But Mr. Collins was not handsome. He was a tall, heavy looking young man of five and twenty. His air was grave and stately, and his manners were very formal. He had recently received ordination and acquired the patronage of Lady Catherine de Bourgh in Kent. He spent most of his first evening talking about Lady Catherine and her daughter Anne de Bourgh.

Lady Catherine was a lady of means and her daughter had poor health. Mr. Collins explained, "Miss de Bourgh's indifferent state of health unhappily prevents her being in Town, and by that means, as I told Lady Catherine myself one day, has deprived the British court of its brightest ornament. Her ladyship seemed pleased with the idea, and you may imagine that I am happy on every occasion to offer those little delicate compliments which are always acceptable to ladies."

Mr. Bennet said, "How happy for you that you appear to have the talent of flattering with delicacy. May I ask whether these pleasing attentions proceed from the impulse of the moment or are the result of previous study?"

Mr. Collins considered the matter, then answered honestly, "They arise chiefly from what is passing at the time, and though I sometimes amuse myself with suggesting and arranging such little elegant compliments as may be adapted to ordinary occasions, I always wish to give them as unstudied an air as possible."

Elizabeth had to bite her lip to keep from smiling and avoided meeting her father's eye as well. Mr. Collins was an absurd, ridiculous man.

"Very sensible," Mrs. Bennet said kindly.

Over the next day, it appeared that Mary's prediction was correct and Mr. Collins was looking for a wife among the Bennet daughters. Mr. Collins seemed to be most interested in Jane, but Mrs. Bennet let him know that she was most likely to become engaged soon, so he shifted his attention to Elizabeth.

Elizabeth did not know how to avoid him but hoped that her lack of encouragement would eventually persuade him to pursue another Bennet daughter. She thought that Mary with her serious turn of mind might be a better companion for him.

The following day, Lydia wished to walk to Meryton, and in the end, Jane, Elizabeth, Kitty and Mr. Collins accompanied her. Mr. Collins spent the walk spouting pompous nothings.

Once in town, Kitty and Lydia looked up and down the street for officers and quickly spied one across the way. It was Mr. Denny and he was speaking with another, taller, handsome gentleman.

"Denny!" Lydia shouted and waved her hand to catch their attention.

Mr. Collins frowned and Elizabeth sighed as her two younger sisters ran to meet them. She, Jane and Mr. Collins followed at a more respectable pace.

Mr. Denny addressed them directly and asked their permission to introduce his friend, Mr. Wickham who had just accepted a commission in their corps.

Elizabeth saw that Wickham had a fine countenance, a good figure, and a very pleasing address.

They spoke briefly about Meryton. His eyes sparkled with wit and intelligence, and dare she presume, with admiration for her?

It was exhilarating and intriguing. Elizabeth had never felt such a wave of male approval before.

As they spoke, the sound of horses drew their notice and Darcy and Bingley were seen riding down the street.

On noticing the ladies of the group, the two gentlemen came directly towards them and began the usual civilities.

Bingley was the principal spokesman and Jane the principal object. He said, "We were on our way to Longbourn to inquire after you, Miss Bennet."

"After both of you, Miss Elizabeth," Darcy added. "I trust you are feeling better?"

"Much better, Mr. Darcy," she said.

Wickham looked at her with concern. "Have you been ill, Miss Bennet?" he asked.

At the sound of his voice, Darcy looked at him sharply.

Elizabeth saw the recognition in both their faces.

Darcy looked horrified and Wickham amused. Wickham made an elaborate bow.

Darcy looked angry, nodded and then turned away.

Bingley saw that his friend was leaving, so he awkwardly took his leave and rode on with him.

Jane frowned, seemingly as confused as Elizabeth, but said nothing.

"Mr. Darcy!" Mr. Collins interrupted. "By any chance was that Mr. Frankenstein Darcy of Pemberley?"

"It was," Elizabeth said.

"Oh, I wish I had known beforehand," Mr. Collins said. "Because I would have introduced myself. Mr. Darcy is the nephew of my patroness, Lady Catherine de Bourgh. I should have spoken to him."

"No, that would be unnecessary," Elizabeth said, knowing that Mr. Darcy would have considered the introduction impertinence rather than a compliment to his aunt. As the superior in consequence, it was up to Mr. Darcy to determine the scope of the acquaintance.

But Mr. Collins disagreed. "My dear Miss Elizabeth, I have the highest opinion in the world of your excellent judgment in all matters within the scope of your understanding, but permit me to explain that a clergyman is equal in dignity with the highest rank in the kingdom, provided that a proper humility of behaviour is at the same time maintained. Rest assured, if I see Mr. Darcy again, I will be sure to speak to him."

Elizabeth knew she could not dissuade him, so the only way to maintain her equanimity was to hope that they never met.

She was pleased, however, that Mr. Denny and Mr. Wickham continued with them, accompanying them to the home of their aunt Mrs. Philips. Lydia invited them to come in and Mrs. Philips spoke through the window, loudly seconding the invitation, but the officers declined and took their leave.

Kitty and Lydia were depressed by the loss of their new acquaintance, Mr. Wickham, but Mrs. Philips promised the girls that they would see him soon. Several of the officers were to dine with the Philipses the next day, and their aunt promised to make her husband call on Mr. Wickham and give him an invitation also, and if the family at Longbourn could come as well, all would be arranged.

As they walked home, Elizabeth discussed with Jane what she had seen pass between the two gentlemen. "Honestly Jane, for a moment it looked as if Mr. Darcy would like to kill Wickham."

"Oh, Lizzy, don't be so dramatic. You sound like Lydia."

"No, it was clear. Wickham was mocking him and Darcy hates him."

"I could not see because of the way the light shone, but I doubt Mr. Darcy hates anyone. After all, he is Mr. Bingley's good friend."

Which had nothing to do with whether Darcy hated Wickham, Elizabeth thought. A man could easily like one man and hate another. But it was a mystery, and she hoped to have a chance to solve it later.

The next night, her family dined with the Philipses and the officers, including Mr. Wickham.

Elizabeth found that her initial impression of Wickham had been correct. He was by far the best among all the officers, far superior in countenance, air and walk. She had always thought Lydia and Kitty silly to be so enamoured by red coats, but she had to admit that Wickham in a red coat gave her heart a little flutter.

She was pleased when he singled her out, choosing not to play whist and sitting by her instead. Lydia sat near them, playing lottery tickets.

"How far is Netherfield from Meryton?" he asked.

"Approximately two miles."

"How long has Mr. Darcy been staying there?"

"About a month. He is a man of very large property in Derbyshire."

"Yes, Pemberley. I know it well."

"I toured the estate as a child," Elizabeth said. "It was a lovely house with even lovelier grounds."

"And I grew up there," Wickham said.

She was surprised.

Wickham added, "You may well be surprised, after seeing the cold manner of our meeting yesterday."

She would have described it more as hot, given the anger in Mr. Darcy's eyes.

Wickham added, "My father was the late Mr. Darcy's steward."

She looked at him closely. She could not recall the details of the miniatures in the sitting room to know if his portrait had been accurate, but she remembered the housekeeper's tale. "Yes, the housekeeper spoke of you."

"Dear Mrs. Reynolds. I was always a favourite with her." He added, "Do you know how long Mr. Darcy plans to be in the country?"

"I do not know. I have heard nothing of his plans."

"Do you know him well?"

"As well as I would like," she said honestly. "I spent nearly a week in the same house with him and found him very disagreeable."

"He has a habit of rubbing people the wrong way," Wickham agreed. "But among the *ton*, he is forgiven because of his wealth. And to be fair, he can please when he chooses. He can pretend to be liberal-minded, just, sincere, rational, honourable, and perhaps at times, even agreeable."

"But you think it is all pretence – not his true nature?"

"Yes, for I am intimately acquainted with his true nature. We were raised almost like brothers. The late Mr. Darcy was my godfather and was very kind to me. He paid for my education and wanted me to make the church my profession. I think Darcy was jealous, resentful. Once his father died, he wasted no time in showing me his true colours."

Elizabeth was fascinated. "In what way?"

"His father had bequeathed me the next presentation of the best living in his gift, but when it became available, Darcy refused to honour it."

"But that is appalling!" she said. "He should be publicly disgraced."

"Not by me," Wickham said. "Out of my love for his father, I will never defy or expose him."

Elizabeth honoured him for such feelings and thought him handsomer than ever as he expressed them. "But it is so difficult to believe," she said. "I knew Mr. Darcy was a proud, arrogant man, but I never thought he would be dishonest."

Wickham shrugged. "Given his origins, perhaps he should not be judged harshly."

"His origins?" Elizabeth frowned. "I don't take your meaning."

Wickham looked about the room to make certain they were not being overheard and he lowered his voice. "It is rumour and conjecture only, but over the years, I have begun to think it is true."

Elizabeth leaned forward, "What is true?

"Very well," he said quietly. "I must explain a few things. Mr. Darcy's father, George Darcy, was one of the best men who ever lived, but he had a flaw. The unchecked pursuit of knowledge."

"Surely the pursuit of knowledge is a worthy endeavour."

"Yes, but that depends on what kind of knowledge. Mr. Darcy was a scientist. He was fascinated by animals and would dissect them. But soon that was not enough. He began to dissect men."

Her eyebrows rose. "Is that not illegal?"

"Yes, he was a grave robber. Not himself exactly. No, as a wealthy man, he could pay men to do his ill deeds for him."

"That is revolting."

"Yes, but that is not all. He studied electricity as well and performed experiments."

She shivered. "I am not certain I wish to hear more, Mr. Wickham."

"I will not dwell on the ghoulish aspects. But have you seen Greenwood?"

"Mr. Darcy's assistant, yes."

Mr. Wickham was amused. "Is that what he calls him? He was a valet to the old Mr. Darcy. But that was a merely a ruse. In actuality, Greenwood is old Mr. Darcy's creation."

"I don't understand."

"They say his body was created from different dead body parts and then re-animated with electricity."

"That is impossible," Elizabeth said. "No one can be brought back to life."

"I am telling you what I have heard; what I believe to be true. Have you seen Greenwood's scars, the obvious combination of different bodies?"

She thought of the scars on his face and his uneven shoulders and arms. "I don't believe you," she said, but part of her rational mind seemed to say, what if it is true?

"And that is not the worst of it. Some say that Darcy is the result of one of his father's experiments as well."

Elizabeth gasped. "How could that be? He does not look anything like Greenwood."

"No. His father improved over time. He gained skills. His first experiment was rushed, but with Mr. Frankenstein Darcy, he took his time."

Elizabeth brought her hand up to her throat, remembering the red scar at Darcy's throat. Had his father sewn the head from one body onto the body of another? It was too ghastly to contemplate.

Fortunately, at this time the whist party broke up and the different guests moved towards Lydia's table, making any additional private conversation impossible.

Mr. Collins mentioned his losses at the card tables, but assured Mrs. Philips that the money was a mere trifle, because his position as rector for Lady Catherine de Bourgh made it unnecessary for him to worry about small expenditures. "Indeed," he said in a loud voice as if addressing the entire room, "when persons sit down at a card table, they must take their chance of these things. And be prepared to pay to play."

Mrs. Bennet beamed as if he had said something profound.

Wickham, overhearing Mr. Collins, asked Elizabeth if her cousin had been long in Lady Catherine's employ.

"No, I believe the appointment is recent."

He nodded. "Lady Catherine de Bourgh and Lady Anne Darcy were sisters, consequently she is aunt to the present Mr. Darcy."

"Mr. Collins said something of the matter."

"Her daughter Miss de Bourgh will have a very large fortune and it is believed that she and Mr. Darcy will marry to unite the two estates."

Elizabeth thought this was information Miss Bingley did not know. It was obvious from the way she flirted with him at Netherfield that she wanted to be Mistress of Pemberley. Elizabeth said, "Do you think Miss de Bourgh has heard the rumours about Mr. Darcy?"

He shrugged. "I don't think it would matter either way. Miss de Bourgh is arrogant and conceited like her mother. If she marries Darcy, it will be for his fortune and prestige. The fact that his father created him in his basement laboratory will not bother her in the slightest."

CHAPTER SEVEN

Elizabeth found it difficult to wait until evening when she could speak to Jane privately about what Wickham had told her about Mr. Darcy.

Later, she was in Jane's bedroom, helping to brush and braid her long hair. They had both changed out of their evening gowns and into white night gowns. Jane listened very politely and when Elizabeth had finished, she said, "Elizabeth, you know it cannot be true."

"But Greenwood."

"He is not the only person to have been injured and horribly scarred. The housekeeper at Pemberley said that Mr. Darcy hired many servants who were maimed. Were they all his inventions?"

Elizabeth nodded. "You are right. It does not make sense. It is more likely that Darcy's father was only a kind man who wanted to help others."

"And if electricity were capable of restoring life, Mr.

Darcy would not be the only one who knew of it."

Elizabeth laughed. "I know. I know. I should not believe Wickham."

"Perhaps he was teasing you, telling you that Gothic tale. You know the way Father sometimes jokes."

"Perhaps," Elizabeth agreed, but she could not help but think of Darcy and wonder. "Wickham did say it was gossip. He does not know for himself."

Jane said, "Like Mrs. Cole and her ghost stories."

Elizabeth sighed. She felt foolish for having been momentarily taken in. She had always prided herself on being a rational creature. It was just that Wickham with his good looks and charm was very persuasive. She would have to tease him the next time she saw him for scaring her with his tales. "I am sorry I even mentioned it to you. I don't want you to have nightmares, too."

"No, I am glad you told me. I would have told you if I had heard such a tale. If true, it would be most alarming." She said, "If you want, I can ask Mr. Bingley about Mr. Darcy."

"No, please don't," Elizabeth said. "It will only make me sound ridiculous. Like a silly chit who is afraid of an evil troll under the bed." As a child, she had read more fairy tales than Jane. "But what of Mr. Darcy refusing to honour his father's wishes as to Mr. Wickham? That part of his story, at least, was very clear."

Jane said, "It is distressing. I think they have both been deceived in some way. Do you think someone may have misrepresented Wickham to Darcy? I cannot believe that Mr. Darcy could be such a villain or that Mr. Bingley would be ignorant as to his friend's true character. And Wickham has such an air of openness. There must have been some sort of misunderstanding."

Elizabeth had to smile at Jane's inability to think poorly of either man. "I am more inclined to believe that Mr. Bingley has been imposed on by Darcy rather than thinking that Mr. Wickham could have made up such a history of himself."

Jane sighed. "I don't know what to think."

"Don't worry about it," Elizabeth said finally. "In time, I am sure the truth will be known." And she was certain the truth would exonerate Wickham and vilify Darcy.

* * *

The next few days were tedious, rain filled days, so there were no trips to Meryton or visits with the Lucases. However, Mr. Bingley did send an invitation for a ball at Netherfield on the following Tuesday, which kept the Bennet daughters busy with anticipation. Both Kitty and Lydia spoke of their desire to dance with Wickham and argued over which of them might dance with him first. Elizabeth said nothing, secretly hoping that he would choose her first.

When she entered the drawing room at Netherfield, she looked in vain for Mr. Wickham among the cluster of red coats. She had dressed with more than usual care and had prepared in the highest spirits to make him fall in love with her. But as she looked, she began to suspect that Bingley had not invited him at Darcy's request.

Lydia asked Mr. Denny about Wickham and was told he had gone to London on business. However, he added, "I do not imagine his business would have called him away just now, if he had not wished to avoid a certain gentleman here."

So Wickham's absence was Darcy's fault, even if he had not done anything directly to cause it. Elizabeth frowned at Darcy, and avoided his approach, choosing instead to talk to her friend Charlotte Lucas.

Her first two dances were then claimed by her cousin Mr. Collins, which further added to her general unhappiness. Mr. Collins, awkward and solemn, apologizing instead of attending, often moved wrong without being aware of it, stumbling over her feet and bumping into the other dancers. Dancing with him was a complete mortification, made even worse by the observation that Mr. Darcy appeared to be watching her. Was he amused by her distress? Cataloguing her lack of coordination with Miss Bingley?

Elizabeth danced next with an officer and had the pleasure of discussing Wickham. Her dance partner said Wickham was universally liked. No one could say that about Mr. Darcy, she thought smugly.

When those dances were over, she returned to Charlotte. To her amazement, she was suddenly addressed by Mr. Darcy who asked her to dance. She was so startled that without knowing what she did, she accepted him. He walked away again immediately and she was left to fret over her own faulty presence of mind.

Charlotte tried to console her. "I dare say you will find him agreeable."

"Heaven forbid!" Elizabeth said, laughing at herself. "To find a man agreeable whom one is determined to hate! Do not wish such an evil upon me."

Charlotte said, "I know you are trying to be clever, Eliza, but do not be a simpleton."

"Meaning?"

"Do not let your fancy for Wickham make you appear unpleasant in the eyes of a man with ten times his consequence."

"Unpleasant?" Elizabeth retorted, offended. She did not know which was worse – that her friend knew how much she liked Wickham – or that she thought she could be influenced by Darcy's fortune. Charlotte was beginning to sound like her mother. "Do you think I give two buttons what that man thinks of me? I will be as unpleasant as I like!" she asserted, but then he was before her, having returned to claim her hand.

Elizabeth blushed, wondering how much he had overheard. If she were truly brave, she would refuse to dance, saying she had a headache or some other ailment, but then she would not be able to dance the rest of the evening.

And before she could create a reasonable excuse, he had taken her hand and led her to the dance floor.

Elizabeth looked at him, tall and straight with broad shoulders and lean, muscular legs shown to advantage in his evening dress. He was more like a Greek God than a monster.

They stood for some time without speaking a word; and she began to imagine that their silence was to last through the two dances. That would be a relief to her, and she was resolved to keep her silence, until it occurred to her that it might be a greater punishment to him to make him talk.

She smiled. "I believe you were wrong, Mr. Darcy, when you thought we did not have enough people in Meryton for a ball."

"Yes, but it is still a small party, compared to similar events in London."

So much for her trying to best him, Elizabeth thought. They were again silent. After a pause of some minutes she addressed him a second time, with, "It is your turn to say something, now, Mr. Darcy. I talked about the dance and you ought to make some kind of remark on the size of the room or the decorations."

He smiled. "What would you have me say? Tell me and I will say it."

"Very well. That reply will do for the present. Perhaps by and by I may observe that private balls are much pleasanter than public ones. But now we may be silent."

His dark eyes seemed intense. "Do you talk by rule then, while you are dancing?"

"Often. It is simpler. Easier."

He smiled. "I suppose it would be unrealistic to discuss deep philosophical matters on a dance floor."

"Yes, if you want me to remember the steps."

"You malign yourself, Miss Bennet," he said, looking deep into her eyes as they began a promenade. "I believe you could dance around me on or off the dance floor."

Was he trying to give her a compliment?

She faltered, taking a wrong step, then corrected herself.

They were both silent till they had gone down the dance, when he asked her if she and her sisters often walked to Meryton.

"Yes. When you met us there the other day, we had just been forming a new acquaintance." *What have you to say to that, Mr. Darcy?*

The effect was immediate. A deeper shade of hauteur spread over his features and for a few moments, he said nothing, as if marshalling his thoughts. Finally, he said in a constrained manner, "Mr. Wickham is blessed with such happy manners as may ensure his making friends. But he is less capable of retaining them."

"He has certainly lost your friendship."

"Yes," Darcy said hotly. "And for several good reasons. I don't know what lies he has told you, Miss Bennet, but I urge you to use great caution around him. Wickham is not what he seems. He is not a good man."

"He says the same of you."

"Then you must be doubly careful in judging either of us."

"Don't worry," she said. "I am a person who gathers evidence before making decisions."

"As you should."

By this time, the dance had ended and he bowed

low over her hand. "I wish you nothing but the best, Miss Bennet," he said, then left her feeling increasingly irritated.

They had not long separated when Miss Bingley came towards her and with an expression of civil disdain, accosted her. "So, Miss Eliza, I hear you are quite delighted with George Wickham! Your sister has been talking to me about him and asking me a thousand questions."

Oh, no, Jane, she thought, hoping she had not mentioned the rumours about Darcy being a monster.

Miss Bingley continued, "I hope you know that he is the son of old Wickham, the late Mr. Darcy's steward. He has treated Darcy in an infamous manner, and Darcy cannot bear to hear George Wickham mentioned."

"Do you know the particulars?" Elizabeth asked.

"No, I would not pry, but I recommend for your sake that you give up your fancy. Mr. Wickham is not worth the trouble."

"How can you say that, when you know absolutely nothing of the matter?" Elizabeth returned.

"I beg your pardon," replied Miss Bingley, turning away with a sneer. "Excuse my interference. It was kindly meant."

And they serve flavoured ice in hell, too, Elizabeth thought rudely.

But then Jane approached her. "Lizzy," she said and pulled her behind a column so they could talk privately. "I talked to Bingley about Wickham. He does not know the whole of their history, but he can vouch for the good will and conduct of his friend."

"As well he should," Elizabeth said. "I would expect no less of him. He is a loyal friend. Does he know of the living?"

"He said he thought it was left to Wickham conditionally only."

"And he received that information from Darcy."

Jane nodded. "Yes."

Elizabeth said, "I have no doubt of Mr. Bingley's sincerity, but he has not changed my mind. I will still think of both men as I did before."

"Oh," Jane added. "One more matter. I asked about Mr. Darcy's scars."

Elizabeth blanched. "Oh, Jane, you didn't."

"Don't worry, I did not refer to the late Mr. Darcy's experiments or any rumours. I merely asked about Mr. Darcy's physical health. I told him we had met years ago at Pemberley."

"And what did he say?"

"He said that he had often gone swimming with Mr. Darcy and that he was in perfect health. He has one scar on his neck and another on his abdomen."

Jane grew red faced at her own bravery. "From the time he was shot."

"Very good," Elizabeth said. "You are a fine sleuth."

Jane blushed. "May I return to Mr. Bingley now? He wants to sit by me at supper."

"Yes, of course." She watched Jane return to Bingley and she spent several minutes in happy anticipation. Bingley was besotted with Jane, there was no denying it. Elizabeth imagined her sister marrying him and settling down at Netherfield. They were two good-natured, well-meaning people and she thought they would find felicity in marriage. Elizabeth did not envy Jane her potential sisters-in-law, but she supposed even Paradise must have a snake or two.

Her mother held some of the same thoughts as she, but unfortunately for Elizabeth's peace of mind, she insisted on sharing them with Lady Lucas, in a voice loud enough to be heard by Mr. Darcy who also sat near them.

"Mr. Bingley is such a marvellous young man," Mrs. Bennet enthused. "It will be so nice when Jane is settled at Netherfield. Only three miles away, so comforting to a mother's heart. And Jane marrying a rich man, can only help my other daughters, by throwing them in the way of other rich men."

Elizabeth was mortified. "Mama, please," she

whispered. "Lower your voice. Mr. Darcy can hear you."

"What is Mr. Darcy to me, pray that I should be afraid of him?"

Elizabeth tried further, but nothing she said could stop her. Finally, after repeating herself two or three times, Mrs. Bennet ate her meal, exclaiming over the quality of the cold chicken and ham.

The remainder of the evening had several additional embarrassments: Mary playing a song that was beyond her skill on the pianoforte, Lydia belching and then giggling, and Mrs. Bennet arranging for them to be the last family to leave.

As they waited for the Longbourn carriage, Mr. Bingley was polite. Miss Bingley and Mrs. Hurst hid their yawns with ill-grace. Mr. Collins bored them all with excessive compliments.

Mrs. Bennet invited Bingley to a family dinner, but he said he was going to Town in the morning, but that he would be back within a week.

"Then you shall dine with us, then," Mrs. Bennet declared. "I will hold you to your promise!"

Elizabeth saw that Mr. Darcy held himself back from the group and wore a solemn expression. *What was he thinking?*

CHAPTER EIGHT

In the morning, Mr. Collins requested a private audience with Elizabeth.

Elizabeth begged her mother not to leave them alone together. "Dear Mama, do not go. Mr. Collins can have nothing to say to me that anybody need not hear."

But her mother ignored her pleas and took Kitty with her. "I insist upon your staying and hearing Mr. Collins." She closed the door behind her, but Elizabeth thought it most likely that she would listen through the door.

Elizabeth sat down and waited, fearing the worst – that Mr. Collins would propose.

And he did. At length. He complimented her on her natural delicacy and modesty that made her dissemble, pretending that she had not noticed his marked attentions. He outlined his reasons for marriage. First, that he believed clergymen should marry as examples for their parishes. Second, that he thought it would greatly add to his happiness. And third, that it was the express wish of his Patroness Lady Catherine de Bourgh that he find an active, useful sort of person, not brought up too high, able to be frugal, and marry her as soon as possible.

He ended by assuring her of the violence of his affection and letting her know that he would never criticize or comment on her meagre dowry once they were married.

Elizabeth listened as long as she could and interrupted as soon as it appeared possible. "You are too hasty, sir," she cried. "You forget that I have made no answer. Let me do so. I thank you for the compliment. I am very sensible of the honour of your proposal, but I must decline."

Mr. Collins smiled as if he had not heard her, or at least had not understood her. He said, "I know it is usual for young ladies to reject the addresses of the man whom they secretly mean to accept when he first applies for their hand. They do this to increase the gentleman's ardour. I am therefore by no means discouraged by what you have just said and shall hope to lead you to the altar ere long."

Elizabeth was flabbergasted. "Please, Mr. Collins,

do me the honour of believing me. I am not one those young women who are so daring as to risk their happiness on the chance of being asked a second time. No, I speak as I find. I am perfectly serious in my refusal. You could not make me happy, and I am convinced that I am the last woman in the world who could make you happy."

"You would make me very happy," he argued. "You are exactly the sort of young woman Lady Catherine wants me to marry."

"Ah, but there you are mistaken, Mr. Collins. I am not. I have read dangerous texts. I believe that women are not merely equal to men, but that in many instances, they are superior. So, I would not make a convenient, compliant wife. I would not follow your lead, unless I believed in its justice and wisdom. I would not be obedient. I would speak up at inopportune times and embarrass you. And if I were angry enough, I would defy you."

Mr. Collins's mouth dropped open. "But. But. The marriage vows!"

"Exactly," she said. "I have serious reservations about the terms. I would have no difficulty promising to love, honour and keep. But in order to obey and serve, the man I marry, if I ever marry, will need to be a paragon. I will need to trust him implicitly with my life."

"And I cannot be that man? Consider my situation in life, my connections with the family de Bourgh, and my relationship to your own. They are all highly in my favour. And think on this. You are a pretty girl but not out of the ordinary, and given your meagre dowry and the limitations of your social sphere, it is unlikely that you will ever receive another offer of marriage. Especially not one as advantageous as my own."

If Elizabeth were not so frustrated and annoyed with him, she might have been amused by his insults. "Thank you, Mr. Collins for your honest assessment of my qualifications. And now, I will take my leave."

She opened the door and almost stumbled over her mother and sisters who were listening outside.

"Lizzy!" her mother exclaimed. "How can you be so obstinate?" Elizabeth stormed out of the house into the garden. Mrs. Bennet turned to Mr. Collins. "Do not worry, sir. I am certain that she can be brought to reason. Let me speak with her father. He will make her do what is right."

Mr. Collins said, "Pardon me, madam, but I have to reconsider the desirability of a young woman who must be forced into the marriage state."

"Oh no, Mr. Collins," Mrs. Bennet assured him. "She will marry you most willingly. I promise."

Elizabeth was walking in the garden, when a servant

called her inside. "You are wanted in the library, miss. By your father."

Elizabeth sighed and straightened her shoulders. She followed after the maid, dreading this next conversation.

Her mother, as expected, was red faced. "Speak to her - your headstrong, foolish daughter," she said shrilly. "Remind her of what she owes to this family. How Mr. Collins can throw us out of this house the minute you are dead."

Mr. Bennet said, "I believe she already knows all that. Do you not, Lizzy?"

"Yes, sir."

"I understand that Mr. Collins has made you an offer of marriage. Is that true?"

"Yes."

"Very well, and this offer of marriage you have refused?"

"I have, sir."

"Very well. We now come to the sticking point. Your mother insists upon your accepting it. Is it not so, Mrs. Bennet?"

"Yes, or I will never see her again!"

Mr. Bennet sighed and shook his head meaningfully. "An unhappy alternative is before you, Lizzy. From this day you must be a stranger to one of your parents. Your mother will never see you again if you do not marry Mr. Collins, and I will never see you again if you do."

Elizabeth could not help but smile with humour and relief. "Thank you, sir."

Mrs. Bennet wailed. "Oh, Mr. Bennet. We shall be on the streets!" She turned to Elizabeth. "You selfish girl. You and your books. What do you know of life? Life requires more than grand thoughts. It requires shillings and pence. Mr. Collins is prepared to save all of us from want. And you are too proud to accept him. I will never speak to you again!" She spoke to Mr. Bennet and stamped her foot. "And I am most displeased with you as well!" She left in a bustle of annoyance, leaving Mr. Bennet alone with his daughter.

Mr. Bennet sighed. "You can see why I choose to stay in the library."

Elizabeth nodded. "I am sorry that I was the cause of disturbing your peace."

He touched her hand. "As long as I do not have Mr. Collins as a son-in-law, I will consider myself fortunate."

* * *

The next few days were unpleasant at Longbourn with Mr. Collins offended and Mrs. Bennet angry. Then

Jane received a letter from Caroline Bingley stating that their entire party was accompanying Mr. Bingley to London, with no plans of returning before Spring.

"How can this be?" Mrs. Bennet cried. "Mr. Bingley promised to be back within a week. Did you do something to offend him, Jane?" She frowned at Elizabeth. "Or you, Lizzy?"

Elizabeth said, "No, nothing, ma'am. Indeed, I expect him to return as promised. Even if his sisters are in Town, that does not mean he could not visit."

"I hope you are right," she said.

And then, as he was preparing to return to Kent, Mr. Collins announced his engagement to Miss Lucas.

"Charlotte Lucas?" Mrs. Bennet exclaimed. "But how can this be? You are in love with Lizzy."

"No, ma'am, I am not," he said clearly. "Miss Lucas has done me the honour of accepting my offer and we are to be married in December. I hope you and your family will join in the celebration."

For a few moments, Elizabeth feared that her mother would spontaneously burst into flames, but she mastered her emotions and said what was proper. But once the man had left, her anger spilled forth. "It can't be true. And if it is true, he has been taken in by Charlotte. She has deceived him, flattering him, using her feminine wiles."

This was ironic considering the fact that she had often considered Charlotte an old maid without any charms.

Mrs. Bennet scoffed. "They will never be happy. I don't know how she can live with herself, deciding to marry a man who only has an estate that is entailed upon him."

"You married Papa," Mary reminded.

"That was an entirely different matter," Mrs. Bennet snapped. "And what were you doing when Mr. Collins was courting Charlotte? If you had been on your toes, you could have caught him."

"Mama," Jane said gently in reproach. "It is not Mary's fault."

"No, but it is grossly unfair," Mrs. Bennet said. "If you do not marry Mr. Bingley soon, Jane, I don't know what I will do with myself. My poor nerves."

Elizabeth and Jane escorted her upstairs where she spent the remainder of the day resting, counting her misfortunes.

The only pleasant event after the Netherfield ball was a morning walk to Meryton. Elizabeth and her sisters planned to visit with their Aunt Philips and they met Mr. Wickham and another officer on their entering the town. The two men attended them and accepted an invitation to join them.

"Why were you not at the ball?" Lydia demanded of Mr. Wickham. "I missed you most terribly."

He smiled. "Don't tell me you moped. I have it on the best information that you danced every dance."

Lydia laughed. "I did."

Later, when the two officers walked them back to Longbourn, Wickham attended to Elizabeth more privately. He explained his absence by saying, "I found that as the time drew near, that I had better not meet Mr. Darcy. I was afraid that if we were in the same room, the same party for so many hours, that it might be more than I could bear. I did not want to be the cause of a scene that would be unpleasant to more than myself."

Elizabeth highly approved of his forbearance. "That was wise. Mr. Darcy seems to have a strong temper."

"He does. He has a resentful nature."

Elizabeth was pleased when they returned to her home for now her parents could make his acquaintance.

* * *

Darcy faced Bingley with a singlestick in his hand. "En guarde," Darcy said and they resumed the beginning position – both of them had stripped down to shirt sleeves and pantaloons. Their feet were bare on the smooth wooden floor. For twenty minutes they fought, lunging and parrying, advancing and retreating. After a whirling cut, Darcy struck Bingley on the side of the head, above his ear. Both men stepped back and lowered their weapons.

Darcy said, "You seem to be distracted today, Charles."

"Forgive me, I am," Bingley said and rubbed the welt on his head. "That Moulinet surprised me. Have you been spending time at Angelo's?"

"Some," Darcy said. As a doctor, he thought it safer to train with a singlestick rather than sword or foil. "Is something bothering you?"

"Nothing but my heart."

Darcy frowned. "Why have you not told me? I would not have taxed you with exercise if I had known you were unwell."

Bingley laughed. "Not my physical heart, Doctor. My emotional heart. I keep thinking of Jane Bennet."

Darcy returned the singlesticks to their cupboard. He said, "I thought you had forgotten her. You have not mentioned her recently."

"No, whenever I do mention her, Caroline starts outlining her flaws. But I think about her constantly. I even dream about her."

"Dreams are foolishness," Darcy said. He dreamt of

Elizabeth, too, but it meant nothing. He motioned to a footman who provided warm damp towels for them to wash their faces and hands, then retreated.

"Perhaps," Bingley agreed. "But I have decided to go back to Netherfield without Caroline if necessary. Do you want to come with me?"

Yes, he did want to go, but Darcy knew that would be dangerous. Elizabeth Bennet had bewitched him as no other woman had bewitched him, and he did not want to stay under her spell. "No, and I don't think you should go, either."

"Why not?"

"Jane Bennet does not like you." Darcy slipped his arms into his waistcoat and buttoned it.

Bingley disagreed. "She likes me."

"She is polite, nothing more. She smiles at you, but she smiles at everyone."

Bingley said, "But what of all the times we spoke together?"

"You are the one who sought her out, correct? Did she ever make an effort to single you out? No. She was merely polite. And she could hardly ignore you when you were her neighbour."

Bingley sat down on a chair, looking downcast. "Have I deceived myself, imagining a tender regard she did not feel?"

Darcy shrugged. "She is not in love with you, that is for certain. She is too cold, too reserved. Her heart will never be touched. The only woman who is in love is her mother. And she is in love with your fortune."

Bingley flinched. "If I proposed, do you think Jane's parents would make her marry me?"

"Most likely."

Bingley hesitated, as if considering that option.

Darcy sat as well and began to put on his stockings. "Don't tell me you would want her under those circumstances. You deserve better, Bingley. Find yourself an open, lively girl who loves you freely. Not that iceberg, Miss Bennet."

"She is not an iceberg!" Bingley protested. "And even if she were, I like icebergs," he added petulantly.

Darcy was struck with a brilliant idea. "Whatever happened to your plans to go to the Arctic Circle?"

"I abandoned them. It was not reasonable."

"Why not? You have the desire, energy and the funds. Besides, now is an ideal time, before you are weighed down with obligations. Caroline could stay with Mrs. Hurst."

Bingley's eyes brightened. "Really? You don't think it is a foolish endeavour?"

"No. You are unhappy, possibly even broken hearted. But nothing contributes so much to tranquilize the mind as a steady purpose – a point on which the soul may fix its intellectual eye. When my father died, I immersed myself in my medical studies. It helped to dull my sorrow."

"You think going to the Arctic Circle will help me forget Jane Bennet."

Yes, just as Darcy knew that taking care of his estate would help him forget her sister. Darcy put on his boots. "Of course," he said. "And the world needs adventurers who chart new paths. Why should you not help discover a new route from the Arctic Ocean to the North Pacific Ocean?"

"Do you think it possible?"

"Why not? What can stop the determined heart and resolved will of man? Eventually someone will find it."

Bingley said excitedly, "There is a man, a Mr. Walton, who is organizing a trip to begin in June."

"Excellent. With preparation, you could accompany him. And I am certain he would appreciate financial support." Darcy stood by a mirror and tied a fresh cravat. He was amused to see that while he had been getting dressed, Bingley still sat, bemused, barefooted with his shirt open at the neck. "I may be willing to support the effort as well," Darcy said.

"You would do that?" Bingley said, amazed.

To keep you out of the clutches of Mrs. Bennet? Darcy thought. "Yes, gladly."

CHAPTER NINE

True to Miss Bingley's predictions, her brother did not return to Netherfield that winter. December was a dismal grey month, only relieved by a visit from Mrs. Bennet's brother Mr. Gardiner and his wife. The Gardiners were Elizabeth's favourite relations. They came to celebrate Christmas and to take Jane back to London for a long visit.

Mrs. Bennet explained how she had been ill used: first by Mr. Bingley who had appeared to love Jane but had then left her, and then by Lizzy, who had refused Mr. Collins. "To think that Lady Lucas has a daughter married, when I have none. Oh, it is too distressing!"

The Gardiners stayed a week and with the Philipses, the Lucases and the officers, there was not a day without its engagement. Elizabeth was glad to see her aunt conversing with Mr. Wickham, sharing memories of Lambton and former friends, including their mutual regard for the late Mr. Darcy. "He was the best of men," Mrs. Gardiner said.

"There are none better," Wickham agreed.

Mrs. Gardiner mentioned their visit in the summer of 1804. Wickham said he had been away that summer, spending time with friends in the North. She said, "I am pleased to hear that the young Mr. Darcy survived his accident."

"I, too," Wickham said. "Although he might not believe it now. We were great friends in our youth, but as adults, we have become almost strangers."

Mrs. Gardiner was intrigued, and on being acquainted with the present Mr. Darcy's treatment of him, she expressed her sincere condolences.

Later she spoke with Elizabeth privately. "I am surprised to hear that Mr. Frankenstein Darcy has treated your friend so abominably. Do you think there may have been a misunderstanding?"

"You sound like Jane," Elizabeth said with a laugh. "No, I think not."

"But when he was young, he had the reputation of being a good-hearted boy, if a little proud."

"I liked him, too, when I first met him," Elizabeth said honestly. "But he has not matured well. He has grown hard and selfish. He thinks he knows everything and that no one is worthy of his approval."

"Did he slight you, Lizzy?"

"Once," she admitted. "But that is not all. He orders his friend Bingley about, and makes pronouncements as if he is addressing Parliament. He is the most infuriating man."

Mrs. Gardiner looked at her closely. "So you do not like him."

"I loathe him."

"Even though he cared for you at Netherfield?"

"Half of that was his showing off his medical skills. Truly, aunt, I only suffered a small bump on my head."

Mrs. Gardiner nodded. "Tell me about Wickham, then."

"He is the most agreeable man I have ever met," Elizabeth said.

"And good looking."

Elizabeth blushed.

"I have seen the way you watch for him, anticipating his arrival," Mrs. Gardiner said. "But I do not want to tease you. You are too sensible a girl to fall in love merely because you are warned against it, and therefore, I am not afraid of speaking openly."

"I am not in love with him," Elizabeth said. *Not yet.*

"No, but if you are not careful, you may find yourself enamoured and that would be a mistake. I have nothing to say against him; he is a most interesting young man; and if he had the fortune he ought to have, I should think you could not do better. But as it is, you must not let your fancy run away with you. A match with him would be most imprudent."

"My dear aunt, this is being serious indeed."

"Yes. You have sense, and we all expect you to use it. Your father can rely on your resolution and good conduct, I am sure."

Elizabeth said, "I will do my best." She hated the fact that she must be on her guard against him, all because of money. Mr. Darcy had a lot to answer to – abominable man!

Within a few days, Jane left with the Gardiners. With her friend Charlotte gone, also, Elizabeth felt lonely and out of sorts. She attended parties and dinners in the neighbourhood with little enthusiasm.

She watched with cynicism as one of her acquaintances, Mary King, inherited a fortune from a distant relation. Mr. Denny had always been her admirer, but after Miss King's good news, Wickham shifted his attentions from Elizabeth to her and within a few weeks, they were engaged.

Kitty and Lydia took his defection to heart and complained bitterly, but Elizabeth kept her thoughts to herself. Why should she be surprised? Marrying for material convenience was the way of the world.

Charlotte had done it by marrying Mr. Collins. Why shouldn't Wickham do the same?

She tried to keep her humour, though, and reminded herself that handsome young men must have something to live on, as well as the plain. And she consoled herself that although she had liked him more than any man she had ever met, she did not love him. She began to think that she might never love any man.

* * *

Elizabeth received weekly letters from Jane, who was enjoying her time in Gracechurch Street. She did not see Mr. Bingley at all, which vexed Mrs. Bennet. After Jane had been in London for a month, she wrote that Miss Bingley had finally made a morning call.

But it was most unpleasant, Lizzy. Caroline was cold and distant, overly formal. She did not mention wanting to see me again. And worse, she told me that Mr. Bingley is planning to go to Russia to join an expedition to go to the North Pole. She says he is a man obsessed with his plans. She says he may be gone for years.

Do not tell mother. She may grieve because he does not return to Netherfield, but that is better than her fearing he has frozen to death.

I feel so foolish for trusting in what was no more than

an idle attraction on his part. Mr. Bingley does not love me. And if he ever did, he has forgotten it now."

Elizabeth crumpled the paper in her hands. She had feared this would be the case, although she had not anticipated a geographic expedition. She felt that much of the blame should fall on his proud sisters, and possibly his even prouder friend.

* * *

In March, Elizabeth travelled to Kent with Sir William Lucas and Charlotte's sister Maria to visit the Collinses. Charlotte had kept up a correspondence between them and very much wanted Elizabeth to visit.

Although Elizabeth wanted to see her friend again, she did not look forward to seeing Mr. Collins. She still found it difficult to believe that Charlotte who had always seemed a sensible young woman had agreed to marry a man she knew was a fool.

Charlotte had said she was not romantic, that all she wanted was a comfortable home. By visiting her, Elizabeth would be able to learn if her friend still felt the same or if she now regretted her choice.

When they arrived at the Parsonage, Mr. Collins and Charlotte appeared at the door and the carriage stopped at the small gate, which led by a short gravel walk to the house. Charlotte welcomed her with the liveliest pleasure, and Elizabeth was more and more satisfied with coming when she found herself so affectionately received. She saw instantly that Mr. Collins's manners were not altered by his marriage. His formal civility was just as it had been. He asked after all her family and then gave her a tour of the house, pointing out every detail for her acknowledgement and praise: the proportions of the room, its aspect, its furniture. She wondered if he did so to make her regret her refusing him, but then thought he could also be motivated to prove to his father-in-law that he was an excellent provider.

The first day there was a busy one, and Elizabeth did not have an opportunity to speak to Charlotte privately until the next afternoon. They sat in a quiet sitting room, undisturbed by Mr. Collins, both of them occupied with needlework. Elizabeth said, "I see you are happy, Charlotte."

"And I see that you are astonished by that," Charlotte returned with sly humour.

Elizabeth smiled. "I am," she admitted.

Charlotte said, "It is very good that I married Mr. Collins and you did not. I don't mind his ramblings or Lady Catherine's interference. I have my own books, my own garden, my own linens. I have three servants. In many ways, marriage is even better than I expected."

She must have had low expectations, Elizabeth thought, but did not say it. "Then I am happy for you."

The next day they were all invited to Rosings Park to dine with Lady Catherine. Mr. Collins carefully instructed them in what they were to expect, so that the sight of such rooms, so many servants, and so splendid a dinner might not wholly overpower them.

Elizabeth thought she would be up to the challenge, whereas poor Maria, only fifteen, looked pale, as if she was going to the guillotine instead of walking half a mile across a fine park.

Rosings Park was a large, beautiful building with many windows. Once inside, Elizabeth was impressed with the ornate decoration: massive paintings on the walls and ceilings, gilded furniture and marble statues. Their footsteps echoed when they entered the main hall.

Lady Catherine was a tall, large woman with strongly marked features which might once have been called handsome. Her air was confident and condescending. She commanded attention and provided the majority of the conversation. Elizabeth amused herself by finding physical resemblances between Mr. Darcy and his aunt. She thought there was a similarity in their eyebrows and the line of their square jaws.

Her daughter, Anne de Bourgh was small, thin and sickly. Her features, although not plain, were insignificant. She spoke very little, except in a low voice to Mrs. Jenkinson, her companion. Elizabeth immediately felt compassion for her, thinking that this little mouse of a young woman would not be up to Mr. Darcy's weight. He would crush her – physically and emotionally. She hoped the rumours of her becoming Mr. Darcy's future bride were false.

After dinner, Lady Catherine asked Elizabeth many questions about her home, her family, how many sisters she had, whether they were handsome, where they had been educated, what carriage her father kept and what had been her mother's maiden name. Elizabeth felt all the impertinence of her questions, but since there was no actual harm in answering, she responded with composure.

Lady Catherine said, "Your father's estate is entailed on Mr. Collins, I think. For your sake," turning to Charlotte, "I am glad of it; but otherwise I see no occasion for entailing estates from the female line."

Elizabeth found it amusing that her mother and Lady Catherine would be of like minds.

Her hostess continued, "Do you play and sing, Miss Bennet?"

"A little."

"Oh, then some time or other we shall be happy to hear you. Do all your sisters play and sing?"

"One does."

"Why did you not all learn? You ought all to have learned. The Miss Webbs all play, and their father has not so good an income as yours. Do you draw?"

"No, not at all."

"What none of you?"

"Not one."

"That is very strange. But I suppose you had no opportunity. Your mother should have taken you to Town every spring for the benefit of masters."

"My mother would have had no objection, but my father hates London."

Lady Catherine frowned as if this was an unreasonable opinion. "Has your governess left you?"

"We never had any governess."

"No governess! How was that possible? Five daughters brought up at home without a governess! I never heard of such a thing. Your mother must have been a slave to your education."

Elizabeth could hardly help smiling as she assured her that had not been the case.

"Then who taught you? Who attended to you? Without a governess you must have been neglected."

"Some might think we were, but I do not. If any of us wished to learn, we never wanted the means. We were always encouraged to read and had all the masters that were necessary. Those who chose to be idle, certainly might." In her family, the older daughters had educated themselves more thoroughly than the youngest two. Kitty and Lydia were quite ignorant.

"That is exactly why you should have had a governess," Lady Catherine argued. "A governess will keep a girl in line with steady and regular instruction."

Elizabeth said, "A greater question, rather than the mode of education, is the purpose and content of education."

Lady Catherine blinked, astonished by her statement. "The purpose of a woman's education is to make her a proper wife."

"By dancing and drawing?"

"It helps a young woman to acquire a husband."

"Yes, but don't you think the acquisition of social skills is less important than the development of a woman's analytical mind?"

"What exactly are you saying, Miss Bennet?"

"I believe that women should receive the same education as men – intellectual and moral training.

Take Plutarch for example. Reading Plutarch taught me high thoughts, he elevated me above the foolish sphere of my own reflections, to admire and love the heroes of past ages. Initially, many things I read surpassed my understanding and experience. As a child, I had a very confused knowledge of kingdoms, the wide extents of country, mighty rivers and boundless seas. But Plutarch showed me new and mightier scenes of action. I read of men concerned in public affairs, governing or massacring their species. I felt the greatest ardour for virtue rise within me, and abhorrence for vice."

"If you want to learn about virtue and vice, you should read the Bible," Mr. Collins said.

"Exactly," Elizabeth said. "But how many women do read the Bible, not just the Psalms? I fear that women without a vigorous education have stunted their ability to think and reason. Accordingly, I believe many men are marrying women who are no more than pretty little children. Ornaments rather than true companions."

"I was never an ornament!" Lady Catherine declared. "Upon my word, you give your opinion very decidedly for so young a person. Pray, what is your age?"

"I have three younger sisters grown up," replied

Elizabeth with a smile. "Your ladyship can hardly expect me to own it."

Lady Catherine scowled at her, no doubt astonished by not receiving a direct answer. "You cannot be more than twenty I am sure. Therefore, you need not conceal your age."

"I am not one and twenty," Elizabeth admitted.

* * *

Sir William stayed only a week at Hunsford, and the next fortnight passed with long walks, talks with Charlotte and dining at Rosings two or three times a week. As Easter approached, Elizabeth was alarmed to learn that Mr. Darcy and his cousin Colonel Fitzwilliam would be visiting their aunt Lady Catherine.

"I had hoped never to see him again."

Charlotte reassured Elizabeth. "I don't think you will have to see him more than once or twice. When Lady Catherine has company, she does not include us as often."

CHAPTER TEN

Darcy did not enjoy visiting his aunt Lady Catherine, but his father had gone every year, and now it was his duty. He had skipped a few visits when he was studying medicine, but now that was concluded, he could not procrastinate any longer. He arranged for his cousin Colonel Fitzwilliam to join him and together they travelled to Kent. At least with the onset of spring, the grounds would be lovely.

The first morning there, Darcy met Lady Catherine's rector, Mr. Collins. He had seen the man before at Netherfield and knew he was a relative of the Bennets. He was alarmed to hear that Elizabeth Bennet was currently visiting Mrs. Collins.

He had hoped never to see her again.

But now that he knew she was there, less than a mile from him, he could not wait to see her again. He told the Colonel that he should go to the parsonage to pay his respects to Mrs. Collins. "She is an acquaintance. I should wait on her."

The Colonel was surprised by his sudden burst of cordiality. "I'll come with you," he said and together the three of them walked back to the Parsonage.

Mr. Collins led the way, talking and waving his hands, telling them how greatly he appreciated the compliment they were giving him by coming to his humble abode.

Once inside, Darcy saw Mrs. Collins, looking neat with a lace cap and a high necked day dress. He paid his compliments and turned to Elizabeth.

His breath caught in his throat and he swallowed hard. He had forgotten how lovely she was with her dark curly hair and her radiant skin. And her eyes brimmed with intelligence. What he wouldn't give to know what she was thinking. He nodded at her. "Miss Bennet," he said formally. "A pleasure to see you again."

Elizabeth merely curtseyed to him, without saying a word other than "sir."

The Colonel entered into conversation directly, asking Mrs. Collins about her family and telling a little of their journey from London.

Darcy wracked his brain to think of something to say. "Mrs. Collins, I notice you have enlarged the vegetable garden and painted the shutters."

"Both on your aunt's suggestion," she answered.

"They look very nice," he said, then damned himself for the stupidity of the remark and was silent for several minutes while the Colonel spoke charmingly.

Elizabeth was also quiet. Eventually he asked about the health of her family and she answered him in the usual way, and after a moment's pause added, "My eldest sister has been in Town these three months. Have you never happened to see her there?"

Miss Jane Bennet? For a moment he panicked. He had not seen her, but he knew she was in Town, for Miss Bingley had told him and he had hidden that knowledge from her brother for fear he would abandon his Arctic journey. Darcy said awkwardly, "I have not been so fortunate as to meet Miss Bennet."

To his relief, Elizabeth pursued the subject no further and they soon after took their leave.

"She's a pretty girl," the Colonel commented, once they were out of earshot of the house. "Is that why you wanted to call?"

"Who is a pretty girl?"

"Not Mrs. Collins or her little sister," his cousin joked. "I am referring to Miss Bennet, as well you know."

"She is pretty," Darcy agreed.

"What is her dowry?"

"Approximately one thousand pounds."

The Colonel sighed dramatically. "Too bad. She would have made a nice armful. Excellent bosom."

Darcy stiffened. "You are vulgar."

"No, merely observant. And don't you dare tell me you haven't thought the same."

Darcy said nothing as they walked back to Rosings Park.

* * *

Within a week, Lady Catherine invited the Collinses and their guests to dine. His aunt was a stickler for fashion and required her gentlemen guests to dress for dinner in breeches, rather than pantaloons which she found vulgar. After he was dressed, Darcy paced about the Library and Greenwood found him. He made an enquiring noise.

"I am fine," Darcy assured him.

* * *

At dinner, Elizabeth found herself seated next to Darcy. She noticed that the footman did not serve him wine, but served him something clear to drink.

"Mr. Darcy, you do not drink wine?" she asked as she sipped her own.

"Rarely. I primarily drink boiled water with a few drops of peppermint oil. It aids the digestion."

"So that is why."

"What?"

She blushed. "You often smell like peppermint."

He looked uncomfortable as well. "Is that bad?"

"No, it is different. But refreshing. My father smells of sandalwood and snuff."

"I hope you like your fish, Darcy," Lady Catherine said loudly.

"Yes, thank you. It is excellent," he said.

Elizabeth noticed that the food Darcy was served was different from the rest of the party, as well.

He saw her looking at him and said quietly. "In order to maintain my health, I must eat smaller meals. Simpler foods. Few sauces or spices."

She wondered if this was because of his injury but did not want to ask. "That is how you developed the diet for Jane when she was recovering."

"Yes. I believe most people would do better by improving their diet."

Colonel Fitzwilliam teased him. "Don't let him fool you, Miss Bennet. For all his talk of diet, he eats a lot of peppermint candies." He turned to his cousin. "It is a wonder you have any teeth left."

Darcy smiled, displaying straight white teeth.

"Periodic eating of sweets is not the problem. Not brushing one's teeth, is."

Colonel Fitzwilliam laughed. "If we are not careful, Miss Bennet, Darcy will bore us all with his strictures on how to live longer. Save your lectures for your patients, Darcy."

"What is that you are saying, Fitzwilliam?" Lady Catherine demanded from her end of the large table. "What is it you are talking of? What are you telling Miss Bennet? Let me hear what it is."

"We are speaking of cleaning one's teeth, Madam," the Colonel said, when no longer able to avoid a reply.

"That is an inappropriate subject for the dinner table," she said firmly. "I do not want anyone to lose their appetite."

She motioned to a footman who entered with a large tray with a pig's head surrounded by fruits and vegetables.

Later in the evening, they all sat in a sitting room and Lady Catherine asked Elizabeth to play something on the pianoforte. "It does not matter what you choose. Anything will do. We do not expect you to have the skill of Miss Georgiana, for you have not had the best tutors."

Elizabeth nodded and walked towards the pianoforte. She saw that Mr. Darcy looked a little ashamed of his aunt's ill breeding.

Lady Catherine announced, "There are few people in England, I suppose, who have more true enjoyment of music than myself, or a better natural taste. If I had ever learnt, I should have been a great proficient."

Colonel Fitzwilliam hurried to his feet, offering to turn the pages for her. "Can you read music?" she asked quietly.

"Well enough. Time will determine if I am proficient."

She smiled at his joke. She liked the Colonel very well. He was not as handsome as his cousin, nor as tall, but he was truly a gentleman with an easy air.

Lady Catherine listened to half a song, then talked, as before, to her other nephew. "I don't think it matters how many mistakes I make," Elizabeth commented quietly to the Colonel. "For no one but you is listening."

"You speak too soon," the Colonel said. "For now Darcy is joining us."

Elizabeth saw that he had walked away from his aunt and had stationed himself to be able to see her face while she played.

She waited for the first convenient pause, turned to him with an arch smile and said, "Do you mean to frighten me, Mr. Darcy, by coming in all this state to hear me? I will not be alarmed even though your sister does play so well. My courage always rises with every attempt to intimidate me."

"I don't think I could intimidate you," Darcy responded. "Even if I wanted to. But I don't think you believe that to be my motive. I have known you long enough to know that you find great enjoyment in occasionally professing opinions which in fact are not your own."

At this, her fingers faltered.

"Practice," Lady Catherine said loudly. "You need more practice, Miss Bennet. You will never play really well unless you practice more."

Elizabeth turned to Fitzwilliam and said lightly, "Your cousin will give you a very pretty notion of me and teach you not to believe a word I say."

"I did not mean that," Darcy said.

"No, it is too late to take it back," she said. "And now I will retaliate by telling your cousin things about you that will shock him."

"I am not afraid of you," he said, smiling.

"You should be."

"Yes, tell me what you have to accuse him of," Colonel Fitzwilliam said. "I would like to know how he behaves among strangers."

"Be prepared for something dreadful," she said, also

joking, but saw a flicker of worry on Darcy's face and wondered if he knew the things Wickham had said about him. But she continued. "When I met Mr. Darcy in Hertfordshire, it was at a ball and he danced only four dances! I am sorry to pain you, but so it was. He danced only four dances, though gentlemen were scarce and more than one young lady was sitting down in want of a partner. Can you deny it, sir?"

"I did not know anyone at the assembly beyond my own party."

"And nobody can ever be introduced in a ballroom," she mocked.

Darcy said, "Perhaps I should have judged better, but I am ill qualified to recommend myself to strangers."

Elizabeth addressed Colonel Fitzwilliam. "Shall we ask your cousin why a man of sense and education, who has lived in the world, is ill qualified to recommend himself to strangers?"

The Colonel said, "I know the answer. It is because he does not apply himself."

Darcy said, "I do not have the talent which some people possess of conversing easily with those I have never seen before. I cannot catch their tone of conversation or appear interested in their concerns."

"My fingers," said Elizabeth, "Do not move over

this instrument as well as I would like but I have always supposed it to be my own fault – because I would not take the trouble of practising."

Darcy smiled and said, "Touché, Miss Bennet. A direct hit. You are perfectly right. I must improve in this area, as well as with my bedside manner."

"Bedside manner?" the Colonel asked, but then Lady Catherine interrupted, asking them what they were talking of. Elizabeth immediately began playing again, effectively ending the conversation.

* * *

Over the next few days, Elizabeth saw Darcy multiple times. He often came with Colonel Fitzwilliam to the Parsonage. She also met him when walking in the woods around Rosings Park. Sometimes he was accompanied by Greenwood, sometimes not. If with Greenwood, they walked much slower and stopped often to enjoy the flowers or to admire the view.

Elizabeth sensed that Greenwood was a little like herself. The sight of what was beautiful in nature seemed to speak to his heart and elevate his spirits.

Darcy never said a great deal, usually nothing more than polite trivialities, but he often stared at her with an earnest, steadfast gaze that unnerved her.

Charlotte teased her, suggesting that Mr. Darcy was

partial to her, but Elizabeth laughed it off. It was much more likely, she said, that he and the Colonel were thoroughly bored at Rosings and were desperately in need of distraction.

One day, when she was walking in Rosings Park, Elizabeth was surprised to meet with Colonel Fitzwilliam. "I did not know that you ever walked this way."

He said, "I have been making my formal tour of the Park as I do every year. I am now on my way to the Parsonage. Are you going much farther?"

"No, I should have turned in a moment."

And accordingly she did turn, and they walked towards the Parsonage together.

"Do you leave Kent on Saturday?" she asked. She and Maria were planning to stay a week longer.

"Yes, if Darcy does not put it off again."

She smiled. "That does not sound like Mr. Darcy. He strikes me as a decisive man."

"Normally he is. Not that I mind. I am completely at his disposal."

"You and Greenwood."

The Colonel smiled. "Fortunately I have a bit more independence than that silent giant."

Elizabeth said, more seriously. "Mr. Darcy seems to take good care of Greenwood."

"He does. He takes care of many people. His servants, his tenants, his friends."

Elizabeth looked at him, surprised. She had not thought of Mr. Darcy in this light. "His friends? I thought he was more likely to order them about."

"No, he looks out for them. Take Bingley for example. I heard that he was in difficulty lately and Darcy helped him extricate himself."

"In what way?"

"A matter of the heart. Darcy saved him from a most imprudent marriage."

"For what reason?"

"There were some very strong objections against the family."

Elizabeth's heart grew cold. He meant strong objections against her family. Darcy did not think Jane was grand enough for his friend. "And what arts did he use to separate them?"

"An Arctic tour," the Colonel said, and laughed. "It seems a bit drastic but definitely effective."

Elizabeth said, "Yes, very few young women would pursue him across the ice."

Colonel Fitzwilliam laughed. "That would make a clever satirical cartoon. A man of means retreating to the North Pole, escaping an army of women in coats and muffs. Can you imagine it?"

"Yes," Elizabeth said, but she did not find it amusing. Who was Mr. Darcy to determine the manner in which Mr. Bingley was to be made happy? And yet, if Bingley was so easily persuaded, perhaps his love for Jane had never been strong.

Either way, she was now completely disgusted with all men, and it took all of her restraint to keep from snapping at Colonel Fitzwilliam. She smiled and changed the subject and said good bye politely at the Parsonage door.

Once inside, she went up directly to her bedroom and closed the door. She let her anger and agitation out with hot tears. Poor sweet Jane. Poor weak Bingley.

Charlotte knocked on the door. "What is it? Do you want to talk?"

"No," Elizabeth answered. "I have a headache."

That was true, not a prevarication. She had an angry headache and she was too upset to go attend tea that afternoon with Lady Catherine. She was afraid that if she saw Mr. Darcy she might do him violence.

Mr. Collins wanted to insist upon her going, but Charlotte intervened. "Let her rest."

"Very well," Mr. Collins said with ill humour. "But Lady Catherine will be displeased."

When they were gone, Elizabeth lay on her bed, wishing she were home at Longbourn.

* * *

Lady Catherine spoke to Darcy privately. "We must talk. Now that you have finished your medical training, it is time for you to settle down."

"I agree," Darcy said. He had been thinking about marriage generally for months, more specifically in the past few days.

"Excellent. Do you want me to arrange the banns or would you rather obtain a special license? I don't think Anne is well enough to marry in London, so she can be married from Rosings."

Darcy said, "You misunderstand me. I am not marrying Anne."

"Of course you are. Your mother and I arranged it when you were both in your cradles."

"Even if that were true, it does not change the present realities. Anne and I do not care for each other in that way."

"A good marriage is based on suitability and similarity, not on romance. Today's youth are too influenced by poetry, and it leads them astray. Our entire family is expecting this marriage. Are you going to disappoint them?"

Darcy tried to be kind. "Aunt, I must marry for my own happiness, regardless of what my family may want."

"But what of Anne? Don't you have any feelings for her?"

"Yes, as a loving cousin, not as a husband. Besides, she is too ill to marry. You must know that. I had my doubts before, but during this visit, I spoke with her. I believe she has consumption."

"No," Lady Catherine said. "That is impossible. No one in our family has had it. And Dr. Harrison has ruled it out. She does not cough up blood."

"There are other symptoms. Pain in her chest. Loss of appetite. Sweating at night. She is ill and she needs better care. A warmer climate if possible."

Lady Catherine said, "But she belongs here, at Rosings. She would not be happier anywhere else."

Darcy had thought for years that her life at Rosings was dismal at best.

Lady Catherine asked, "How long does she have?"

"I don't know," Darcy said honestly. "A year, possibly two."

"Then marry her," Lady Catherine urged. "Make her last days happier. You can choose whomever you want as your second wife."

"I cannot."

"Will not is what you mean," Lady Catherine said angrily. "How can you be so selfish?"

Darcy bowed his head. There was nothing more to be said. "Colonel Fitzwilliam and I will leave tomorrow."

* * *

Half an hour later, Elizabeth heard the door-bell, and thinking it might be Colonel Fitzwilliam calling to enquire after her, she came downstairs.

But instead of the Colonel, it was Mr. Darcy. "May I speak with you?"

CHAPTER ELEVEN

Elizabeth let him in the room; it would have been impolite to refuse. She sat down on a couch and looked up at him.

"Mrs. Collins said you were ill," he said bluntly.

"A headache only. I am fine."

"Your injury has not continued to bother you?"

For a moment she did not know what he was referring to, then she remembered her fall at Netherfield. "No, absolutely not. I rarely have headaches. I believe I am completely recovered."

"I am glad." He sat down for a few moments across from her and then getting up walked about the room.

Elizabeth was surprised by his agitation but did not comment.

After a silence of several minutes he came towards her and blurted out, "In vain have I struggled. It will not do. My feelings will not be repressed. I have love in me the likes of which you can scarcely imagine. You must allow me to tell you how ardently I admire and love you."

Elizabeth was so astonished, she was momentarily silent, unable to respond.

He must have seen her silence as encouragement, so he continued. "I believe I started falling in love with you at the Meryton Assembly and by the time you came to Netherfield, I was completely smitten. I knew it was foolishness. I knew your family situation was beneath my own and that my family and friends would disapprove. I told myself that what I felt for you was merely a passing fancy, a momentary lust, but I found myself thinking of you night and day. I could not tear my eyes away. It was not only your physical beauty that enchanted me. It was your mind, your courage, your laughter. You saw how I hovered, anxious to hear every word from your mouth.

"I was a man obsessed. My feelings for you were unreasonable and unrelenting. The ball at Netherfield was excruciating. Internally I was at war with myself. I wanted to sweep you into the gardens and declare myself then, but I knew it was wrong and that I would regret succumbing to my passions. I left Hertfordshire, vowing never to return."

Good heavens, Elizabeth thought. Mr. Darcy loved

her? Once she was over the shock of his disclosure, she was momentarily sorry for the pain her rejection would cause, but as he continued to talk, she grew increasingly offended by his verbiage.

He said, "My attachment to you was so strong that I could not forget you. And when I saw you here, I knew that I could fight my love no longer. I hope you will now put me out of my misery and reward my undying love by accepting my hand in marriage."

As he spoke, Elizabeth could easily see that he had no doubt of a favourable answer.

"Please speak, dearest Elizabeth, and relieve my fears before they overtake me."

He spoke of apprehension and anxiety, but his countenance expressed real security, which exasperated her.

She had never thought Mr. Darcy to be similar to Mr. Collins, but they were both single-minded, arrogant men who thought all they had to do was ask and a woman would immediately agree to give up her future.

Elizabeth drew her breath in sharply and strove to compose herself. "In such cases as this," she said finally, "I believe it is the established mode to express a sense of obligation for the sentiments avowed, however unequally they may be returned. But I cannot thank you for your offer. I have never desired your good opinion and you have certainly bestowed it on me unwillingly. I am sorry to give pain to anyone, but it has been unconsciously done, however, and I hope it will be of short duration."

Mr. Darcy had been leaning against the mantelpiece with his eyes fixed on her face. As she spoke, he first looked surprised, then angry. He struggled for composure and said, "And this is all the reply to which I am to have the honour of expecting! I might, perhaps, wish to be informed why, with so little endeavour at civility, I am thus rejected."

"Why should I be civil when you are not? You said you fell in love with me, against your will and your better judgment. Was that civil? Was that kind? What woman in her right mind would take a man who cannot even propose without insulting her? And that is not all, how could I consider a man who has been the means of ruining, perhaps forever, the happiness of a most beloved sister?"

At her words, Darcy changed colour.

She continued, "I have every reason in the world to think ill of you. You sent Bingley to the Arctic, separating him from Jane, possibly putting his life at risk. Can you deny it?"

"I have no wish of denying that I did everything in

my power to separate my friend from your sister and I rejoice in my success. Towards him I have been kinder than towards myself."

Elizabeth's hands formed fists. He was insufferable. "But it was not just this matter that makes me dislike you. Wickham told me of your unfair treatment of him. How can you justify that?"

"You take an eager interest in that gentleman's concerns."

"And who would not? His misfortunes –"

Darcy made a rude noise. "Tell me, what are his misfortunes other than those of his own making?"

"You have reduced him to his present state of comparative poverty and yet you blame him. You treat him with contempt and ridicule."

"If you knew him as I do, you would share that contempt."

"No, I would not," she said hotly. "The only contempt I have is for you. From the moment you came to Hertfordshire, your manners have shown you to be arrogant and conceited with no compassion or regard for your fellow man."

"And this is your opinion of me? My faults according to your calculation are heavy indeed. But perhaps, you could have overlooked them if I had not hurt your pride by expressing my honest concerns for your family and connections. Should I have lied and flattered you?"

"Not at all. Changing the mode of your declaration would have made no difference. Wickham told me rumours that you were a monster, one of your father's medical experiments. I don't think that is true. I believe you were born a gentleman but unfortunately your attitudes and behaviour have made you act like a monster. I would never marry you, not if you were the last man in the world. I would rather marry Greenwood!"

Darcy's face grew pale. "You have said quite enough, madam. I perfectly comprehend your feelings and have now only to be ashamed of what mine have been. Forgive me for taking up so much of your time and accept my best wishes for your health and happiness."

With these words, he bowed and hastily left the room.

Elizabeth put her hand to her forehead. Her headache was throbbing now. She sat down, trying to calm her racing thoughts.

Darcy loved her? He had loved her for months? That was impossible, and yet she knew he was sincere. Sincerely conceited. Sincerely infuriating.

She did not know if she should be gratified that

such a proud man had lowered himself to think of her or if she should be horrified.

He had expressed no remorse for harming Jane or Wickham.

It did not matter that he had professed an ardent love for her. He was a horrid man and she hated him.

So why did she want to cry?

* * *

In the morning, Elizabeth felt no better. Her eyes were red from crying the night before, and she slipped from the Parsonage after breakfast to take a walk. She needed to ease her rabid thoughts and she had often found fresh air and solitude to be restorative.

She walked quickly, bonnet in hand rather than on her head.

Within a few minutes, she saw that she had mindlessly chosen one of her favourite walks, one where Darcy had sometimes met her. She turned on her heel to choose another path, but then she heard him call out. "Miss Bennet!"

She was tempted to run, but did not know if in his arrogance he would follow her. She turned back around to face him.

He hurried to approach her. He did not look like himself. His hair was standing up, his clothes dishevelled as if he had slept in them – or if he had not slept at all. His cravat was loose and the lowered fabric displayed hints of the scar at his throat – pink now instead of the red it had once been.

"Mr. Darcy," she said formally.

"Forgive my intrusion," he said, equally cool, his words in direct contrast to the blazing of his eyes as they looked at her. "I have been walking in the grove for some time in the hope of meeting you. My cousin and I are leaving Rosings Park today."

"And you wanted to say good bye?"

"I wanted to give you this." He held out a letter. "Would you do me the honour of reading it?"

She hesitated. They both knew that it was improper for a young woman to receive a letter from a young man she was not engaged to.

But there was no one to see their breach of societal norms. And she did want to read it. She took it from his hand.

"I rely upon your sense of justice," he said.

She turned. "Good bye, Mr. Darcy."

"I cannot say good bye to you, Miss Bennet. Au revoir."

She forced herself not to turn back, not to watch him as he walked away, although she stood silent, listening to the sound of his boots on the damp ground. She stood like one of the statues in Netherfield Park, looking down, waiting for him to be gone.

Finally, she trusted that she was alone and she tore open the letter. His handwriting was thick and dark.

Be not alarmed, Madam, on receiving this letter, by the apprehension of its containing any repetition of those sentiments, or renewal of those offers, which were last night so disgusting to you. I write without any intention of paining you, or humbling myself, by dwelling on wishes, which for the happiness of both, cannot be too soon forgotten.

"Good," Elizabeth said out loud, as if he was there before her. If he tried to change her mind, he would be unsuccessful. She continued to read.

I write only to respond to the offences that you laid to my charge yesterday.

The first, that regardless of the sentiments of either, I detached Mr. Bingley from your sister.

I did separate Bingley from your sister. I was the one who suggested the Arctic adventure. Bingley had expressed an interest in it before, and I thought the frozen wastelands better than marriage into your family. As much as I admire you and your sister and acknowledge your sense and decorum, you must admit that the remainder of your family are often vulgar, displaying a total want of propriety.

At the time, I thought your sister did not care for Bingley. Her look and manners were open, cheerful and engaged, but without any symptom of peculiar regard. I thought she was indifferent. I also did not think her affection for him, if indeed there was any, could be of any depth considering the brevity of their acquaintance. They had only known each other a few short weeks, insufficient, surely, to be the basis for a lasting relationship.

I acknowledge your superior knowledge of your sister's feelings, and to the extent that I have caused her pain, I apologize. However, once you know all, I believe my actions will have been like a pungent medicine. Distasteful at first but ultimately beneficial for the patient.

Bingley is a mercurial man. I have seen him fall in and out of love many times. I did not think his affections for your sister would last beyond a month. Trust me, it is better for him to abandon your sister now than to have her develop even deeper feelings for a man who will flirt but never propose.

Elizabeth drew her breath in sharply. Mr. Darcy was correct, in part, for his words were like medicine, but more like a bandage ripped from a wound that had started to heal.

She herself had wondered at Bingley's constancy. He seemed so amiable, so easily pleased. Perhaps Darcy did know him better and he would have broken Jane's heart. But it was still high-handed of Darcy to intervene. And his justification – that the Arctic wasteland was better than her family – that stung.

He said they were vulgar, but surely that was his pride speaking, for he was more accustomed to people of high fortune. But then she remembered the Netherfield Ball and the embarrassment she had felt, wishing her family were better behaved. She forgave her family because she loved them, but he had no reason not to judge them harshly.

She continued to read.

As for Wickham's accusations, let me begin with my father. He was a brilliant, kind man, and I hope that one day I may be half as good. My father was a scientist and yes, he did dabble in areas of science that are deemed dangerous. He did perform dissections, first with animals and later with human cadavers, but that is the way he learned. The current laws regarding dissection are antiquated and need to be reformed. Changing those laws will be one of my few political efforts. I believe that the pursuit of scientific knowledge is more important than the superstition and fears of the past.

My history with George Wickham is a complicated one. As children, we grew up together. We were friends, but over the years, I learned that he was not to be trusted. He was dishonest and would take advantage whenever he could. My father only saw the good in him, but I, for many years his best friend, could not help but see his vicious propensities, his total want of principle. When we started college, he was left unchecked and seemed to seek out everything base and immoral. One summer I visited with my uncle the Earl of Matlock. When I returned to Pemberley, Wickham was different. I learned that he had met with an accident in Lambton and had been ill for several months.

Physically, he was recovered, but it seemed to me as if the anger that had always been a part of his character was augmented. He seemed more impulsive. But then, there were moments when he appeared to be the same, and I thought I was mistaken. But our friendship, which had been increasingly precarious, ended.

When my father died, Wickham appeared to claim his legacy of 1000 pounds and asked for an additional 3000 pounds in exchange for the promise of the living. I readily agreed because I knew that given his proclivities he should not be a clergyman.

How he spent the next three years, I know not, but I assume he wasted the money and did not study the law as had been his professed plan.

At this, Elizabeth paused and reread the previous paragraphs. Could this be true? Wickham had mentioned the living, but never that he had been compensated. She continued.

Last summer, he tried to elope with my younger sister Georgiana who was only fifteen at the time. This story pains me for several reasons. First, that I put my sister in danger. I was such a careless guardian that I was deceived by Mrs. Younge, the woman I had hired to be her companion. I later learned that Mrs. Younge was in conspiracy with Mr. Wickham.

Fortunately, I was able to stop them. I arrived the day before they were to elope. Georgiana, not wanting to keep the news from me, confessed all.

And I confronted Wickham.

The recollection of our conversation also gives me pain, as I will explain. I will never forget his words to me.

"Why shouldn't I marry her?" he demanded. "I love her and she loves me. Rest assured, Darcy, she will marry me, it is only a matter of time. When she attains her majority, I will wed her."

I then had to tell him the secret that had weighed heavily on my heart for four long years. From my father's statements on his deathbed I believed that Wickham was his illegitimate son.

"No!" Elizabeth breathed out, shocked, then continued to read.

I said to him, "Even if I thought you were worthy of her, you cannot. You are her half-brother."

Georgiana fainted and Wickham was astonished. "So that is why," he said finally.

"Why what?" I demanded.

"Why your – I mean our – father saved my life." At my confusion, he added, "I am his creation, just like Greenwood."

It took me a few moments to understand what he was saying. I had known for several years that my father had created Greenwood from several bodies and had reanimated him with electricity. "I don't believe you."

He then showed me his scars – faint, but clear. Wickham had been attacked in the woods outside Lambton. My conjecture is that a local father had taken revenge for Wickham despoiling his daughter. He had been viciously hacked to pieces with pitchfork and pruning shears.

Greenwood's creation had been done quickly and the available body parts had been inferior. But for Wickham, my father took extra pains. He purchased premium corpses from the North and kept them on ice. He worked for days, combining the best of four bodies so that Wickham, when he was re-animated, looked almost perfect.

I was horrified, and yet fascinated by the work my father had done. He was a genius, but I believe it was a mistake to bring Wickham back to life.

"It is not fair," Wickham told me. "I did not ask to be put together like an anatomical puzzle. Your father gave me life and he owes me a living."

I could not refute his charges. My father had told me the same on his deathbed – that Wickham was my responsibility now. But unlike Greenwood, Wickham had looks and charm and the natural abilities to be independent.

Naturally, Wickham now wanted money in exchange for secrecy about his parentage.

"There is no proof," I said. Wickham's birth records listed his mother's husband as his father. "Indeed, I believe my father must have had his own doubts or he would have left you more than just the living."

"Then why do you believe it?"

In the end, I gave him another 2000 pounds with the hope that I would never see him again.

You saw our next meeting in Meryton.

I do not know what lies he has told you, but like most successful liars, I assume it has been a combination of truth and falsehood. I do not fault you for believing him. Ignorant as you have been of our history, detection could not be in your power, and suspicion certainly not in your inclination.

You may wonder why all this was not told to you last night, but I was not then master enough of myself to know what could or ought to be revealed.

I do not talk of my father's work. It only gives rise to gossip and would lead other, less scrupulous scientists to try to duplicate his efforts.

As for Georgiana's near elopement, you can speak to Colonel Fitzwilliam for confirmation. As her co-guardian with me, he knows of that matter, although not the specifics of Wickham's re-creation.

"Good heavens," Elizabeth breathed out. For a moment, she held the letter against her breast as if it could calm the frantic beating of her heart.

Wickham Darcy's half-brother? Wickham like Greenwood? Both of them creations of Darcy's father? It was impossible to believe. Wickham was handsome and strong. But from what Darcy wrote, he had been re-created like Greenwood. She returned to the letter.

Given this history, you must wonder if I was re-animated as well. I was not. The scar on my neck has a more plebeian cause. When I was a young man, during one of my first visits to London, I was encouraged to go to a gambling club. I won a large sum and decided to walk back to Darcy House in the early hours of the morning without my companions who continued to drink and game. I was attacked from behind by footpads and my throat was slit. I was left for dead.

Fortunately, I was found quickly and the wound was superficial. It was hastily repaired by a housekeeper, hence its untidy seam. It is a daily reminder to me not to drink to excess and not to gamble. My father had warned me that there is safety in righteous living, and I have tried to follow his warning and live by his excellent example.

I also have a scar on my abdomen from when I was shot at Pemberley. I realize now, in the writing of this letter that I have never thanked you sufficiently for your actions that day. If it were not for your quick thinking and bravery, I would have died on that path.

My father often mentioned you, wishing that he could have thanked you himself.

This is the end of my response. I hope that if it has not changed your opinion of me, that at least it has given you knowledge for you to face your future wisely.

I shall endeavour to find some opportunity of putting this letter in your hands in the course of the morning. I will only add, God bless you.

Frankenstein Fitzwilliam Darcy

CHAPTER TWELVE

Elizabeth did not know what to think or how to act. She walked for half an hour, stopping often to reread Darcy's letter.

Who was the true monster? Wickham or Darcy?

She had never doubted Darcy's veracity, merely his judgment. His letter, although it contained facts and sentiments she would rather not consider, was logical and had the air of truth.

He had told her that she could ask Colonel Fitzwilliam to confirm the story that Wickham had tried to elope with Darcy's younger sister.

This put Wickham's attentions to Miss King in a different, totally mercenary light. And the details about the living, whose version should she believe? She realized now how indelicate Wickham had been to share his history with her when they first met. She remembered how he had said he would never expose

Darcy because of his love for his father, yet as soon as Darcy left town, Wickham had spread his tale of injustice.

What did she know of Wickham, other than the fact that he was Mr. Denny's friend? She knew nothing of his past.

But with Mr. Darcy, she had met him when he was a young man and had been impressed by him. She and her aunt knew of his family. Bingley vouched for him. As a doctor, he had cared for her and Jane at Netherfield, treating them both with respect.

Elizabeth grew absolutely ashamed of herself. She could not think of Darcy or Wickham without feeling that she had been blind, partial, prejudiced and absurd.

She had acted despicably. She had always prided herself on her discernment and had thought poorly of Jane for being so uniformly generous. But she, in her vanity, had distrusted Darcy and believed Wickham's lies.

And why? Because Wickham had flattered her and Darcy had not.

She felt as if until this moment, she had never known herself.

And what she saw, she did not like. She must strive to be more reasonable, less impulsive.

She thought of Jane and Bingley. Darcy may have

been mistaken as to Jane's feelings, but Jane was reserved in public. Elizabeth could understand how Darcy might have misjudged her. And as for Bingley, Darcy knew him much better than she. There was no way to know if Bingley's regard for Jane would have matured into something lasting.

She reread the last section of the letter. How embarrassed she was to remember what she had said about preferring Greenwood to him and yet, Darcy did not hold a grudge. His closing had been kindness itself.

Elizabeth sighed and held the letter to her lips. She did not want to see Darcy again. Ideally, she hoped that he would go back to London, so she could forget him and her foolishness.

She wandered along the lane for two hours, giving way to every variety of thought and re-considering events, determining probabilities and reconciling herself as well as she could to the change in her perspective.

* * *

Nothing could be more painful to the human mind than, after the feelings have been worked up by a quick succession of events, the dead calmness of certainly which follows and deprives the soul of hope.

Elizabeth did not want him and Darcy felt the full weight of despair.

But he could not remain inactive. As he prepared to leave Rosings, he spoke with Greenwood and his valet Bowles. He tried not to think of Elizabeth reading his letter. Would she believe him? Would his words change her heart?

Before Elizabeth, he had thought of marriage as a practical matter. He had made a list of the qualities he had been seeking in a wife. But then Elizabeth had changed him, just as a bolt of lightning could turn sand into glass.

He now knew that he did not merely want a wife – he wanted a woman who would provide intimate sympathy with a like mind. Someone who would see him as he was and accept him wholeheartedly.

He had thought, he had hoped that Elizabeth was that woman, but she had rejected him, and now he feared that he would never find happiness again.

Darcy met briefly with Anne, who sat with Mrs. Jenkinson in one of the gardens. Anne was wrapped in a heavy shawl despite the warm weather. She reassured him that she did not want to marry him, even if her mother insisted. "I am too tired to marry anyone," she said with a little smile.

"I will write to you," Darcy promised and kissed her hand in farewell.

He also asked Lady Catherine's housekeeper if he

could speak to her ladyship's maid Miss Ellis. Miss Ellis had burned her cheek from an accident with a curling iron a week before he arrived. Anne's doctor had dismissed the injury as not important at the time with a terse, "Just put butter on it." But the housekeeper, when learning of Darcy's medical training, had asked him to look at it.

Miss Ellis was a thin woman in her late thirties. She wore her hair pulled back in a tight bun and a black dress that buttoned high on her neck.

The burn was dark red and blistered, but Darcy was pleased to see that it did not appear to be infected.

"Have you had a fever?" he asked.

Miss Ellis shook her head. "No, sir."

"Very good. Are you back to your duties?"

"No, sir. Her ladyship does not want to see me until I am healed."

Darcy nodded. Lady Catherine did have strict standards for her servants. "The burn should be healed in another week or two."

"Thank you, sir. Will there be a scar?"

"I am afraid so," Darcy said.

"Oh, no." Tears filled the woman's eyes.

He said, "Hopefully it will not be very noticeable."

The woman shook her head. "No, sir. I am not worried about that, but her ladyship said she will dismiss me. She does not want anyone ugly to attend her."

Darcy swore under his breath. He would wager that the injury itself had been her ladyship's fault. She was often impatient and had been known to strike her servants. He had not planned to speak to his aunt privately before he left, but he left the maid to find her.

Lady Catherine was in a sitting room, embroidering. "Darcy!" she said happily, setting her needlework aside. "Have you reconsidered marrying Anne?"

"No, ma'am, I have not," he said coolly.

"Then I have nothing more to say to you."

Darcy stood his ground. "I am here as your maid's doctor. Miss Ellis."

"Oh, yes, the woman who used to style my hair. What is the problem? I am temporarily using Anne's maid and will hire someone from London. It is none of your concern."

"Miss Ellis says you will dismiss her if she is scarred."

"Naturally I will dismiss her. Perhaps I would not mind if she worked in the kitchen or as a scullery maid, but I don't want to look at that face every night as she brushes my hair. And she does not look strong enough to work in the kitchen, so yes, I will dismiss her. With a reference of course, although I don't think she deserves one for being so clumsy. Thank you for reminding me. I will see that the housekeeper takes care of it today." She turned away, still angry with him. "I find it difficult to believe that you care more for this servant than your cousin."

"And I find it difficult to believe that as Mistress of Rosings Park, you do not take better care of your own people."

Colonel Fitzwilliam was surprised when Miss Ellis joined them for their journey. "What's this?" he asked.

"I have hired a new lady's maid for Georgiana."

The Colonel spoke to him a few yards away the carriage, where they would not be heard. "What are you doing? Isn't Greenwood enough? You cannot hire everyone who is disfigured."

"No, but I can hire one person today." It was similar to practising medicine. He could not save the world, but he could take care of the person who was before him. One person at a time.

Colonel Fitzwilliam shook his head. "I think you are trying to show us up. Make the rest of us feel guilty."

"No, it is not a matter of guilt. It is a matter of right and wrong. That poor woman should not lose her position because of Lady Catherine's temperament."

"You think she caused the accident?"

"I do."

Colonel Fitzwilliam said, "Don't ever join the army, or there won't be a single empty bed at Pemberley."

"Don't worry, I won't turn Pemberley into a hospital."

"Or Darcy House?"

"No." But he had thought of starting a small private hospital in London. And now that the woman he loved had rejected him, the prospect had even more appeal. He must do something of value with his life or he would go mad with disappointment.

* * *

When Elizabeth arrived back at the Parsonage she learned that Mr. Darcy and Colonel Fitzwilliam had called to take their leave while she was walking. They had stayed for only a few minutes.

Mr. Collins reported that he had seen their carriage leave an hour later. He walked over to Rosings to spend time with Lady Catherine but returned to say that her ladyship was feeling poorly and did not want company. "She misses her nephews most acutely."

The next day, Charlotte spoke to Elizabeth in her private sitting room. "I have heard something from my maid, and she heard it from the great house."

Elizabeth frowned. "Are you certain you want to repeat servants' gossip?"

"Sometimes servants' gossip is true," Charlotte said. "And it is a wise woman who is aware of the rumours, whether she believes them or not."

Elizabeth said, "So what is it?"

"It is about Mr. Darcy. You know he is meant to marry his cousin Anne."

"Yes." She had heard that from both Mr. Collins and Wickham, but since he had proposed to her, she thought it did not matter what others thought. He obviously did not consider himself tied to his ill cousin.

"Well, during this recent visit, Mr. Darcy refused to marry her. They heard him and his aunt arguing. And then you will never guess what happened next."

Elizabeth held her breath. Did anyone know that he had proposed to her? "What?"

"He took her ladyship's maid with him to London. A woman who used to style Lady Catherine's hair."

This was so completely not what she expected to hear that Elizabeth gasped. "No."

"Yes, and some say she is with child."

"Charlotte, you can't believe that," Elizabeth said sharply. "That is so out of character. Mr. Darcy may be disagreeable, but he is not dissolute."

Charlotte said, "Mr. Collins says that most gentlemen of the *ton* have mistresses."

Elizabeth had heard her mother and Mrs. Philips whisper about this as well, but she could not believe it. Especially not when he claimed to love her. *You must allow me to tell you how ardently I admire and love you.*

"I don't believe it," she said staunchly.

Charlotte looked at her closely. "It seems you like Mr. Darcy after all."

* * *

The journey home to Longbourn was tedious, relieved by a short stay with Mr. and Mrs. Gardiner. Jane joined Elizabeth and Charlotte's sister Maria, and together they all travelled back to Hertfordshire. Elizabeth wished to talk to Jane, to tell her about Mr. Darcy's proposal, but she thought she should wait until they were home. As they entered Hertfordshire, they drew near an inn where Mr. Bennet's carriage was to meet them. They saw Kitty and Lydia looking out of a dining room upstairs. They had come as a surprise to meet them.

They had arranged for a table with cold meat and salad, but needed to borrow money to pay for it because they had spent theirs at a milliner's shop nearby.

Lydia had bought a bonnet that Kitty said was ugly. "I agree," Lydia said. "But it was the best in the shop. I shall pull it to pieces as soon as I get home and see if I can make it up any better. Not that it will matter, once the regiment has left."

"What is this?" Jane asked.

"The regiment are leaving Meryton for Brighton and will be gone within a fortnight."

This seemed like a blessing to her family, Elizabeth thought. Without the soldiers to distract them, her sisters might grow up to be reasonable young women.

Lydia said, "They are going to be encamped near Brighton and I do so want Papa to take us there for the summer! Mama thinks it an excellent notion."

Elizabeth glanced at Jane who seemed to have similar thoughts to her own. If Lydia and Kitty could not behave with one regiment of militia, how would they act with a whole campful? "What does Papa say?"

"Oh," Lydia said suddenly. "I can't believe I forgot. I should have told you this straight away. It is about Wickham."

Elizabeth steeled herself. She was not looking forward to seeing him again, now that she knew more about him.

"Miss King was murdered!" Kitty interrupted with ghoulish satisfaction.

"Murdered!" Elizabeth repeated, aghast.

"Yes," Lydia said. "And I'll tell the story, Kitty, for I heard it first."

"What happened?" Jane asked.

"Miss King and her uncle were taking a trip. They stopped at an inn and in the middle of the night, they were robbed and murdered."

"Good heavens. What has been done about it?"

"The magistrate is gathering evidence."

Kitty said, "They say their throats were cut."

"No," Lydia argued. "I heard it from Colonel Forster's wife. The uncle's throat was cut, but Mary King was stabbed in the heart."

Jane shuddered. "I cannot bear to hear this."

"No," Lydia said. "I should have waited until after we had all eaten."

"But what of Mr. Wickham?" Jane asked. "The poor man."

"I know," Lydia said. "He is heartbroken. I did not think he cared for Miss King before. Who could about such a nasty little freckled thing?"

"Lydia!" Elizabeth said sharply. She was chagrined to realize that although she would never have said such a thing about Miss King out loud, she had previously thought it.

Lydia shrugged. "I know I should be kinder because

she is dead, but that is what I thought, and I was wrong. I think Wickham really loved her. He is so distraught; Colonel Forster is talking about giving him leave."

Elizabeth did not know what to say. As much as she disliked Wickham, she could not help but sympathize with the horror of his fiancée's death.

Once home they were met by Mrs. Bennet, who was pleased to see that Jane was as beautiful as ever. Mr. Bennet told Elizabeth, "I am glad you are come back, Lizzy."

The next morning, Elizabeth arranged to take a walk with Jane, so she could tell her about Mr. Darcy's proposal. They walked through the fields, towards Netherfield.

Jane was astonished when she heard Elizabeth's news. She agreed that Mr. Darcy's mode of courtship was lacking, but she was sympathetic to his pain. "The poor man. What he must be feeling."

"You don't think I should have accepted him?"

"No, not if you don't love him," Jane said. "I am just sorry for him."

"I am sorry for him, too." Elizabeth said. "But I doubt he will grieve long. His natural pride will remind him of the many reasons why I would make a most unsuitable wife."

Jane said, "I hope you are right."

"The only part of our conversation I regret is having spoken so warmly of Wickham."

"You are his friend. Of course you spoke warmly of him."

"But I am not his friend now," Elizabeth said and told her of Darcy's letter. She did not tell Jane that Wickham had been re-created from four bodies and reanimated because she did not want to horrify her, and she thought that Darcy would not wish it. He did not want others to learn about his father's work. She also did not tell her his suspicions that Wickham was his half-brother. Elizabeth did, however, tell Jane about the living and about the near elopement with Georgiana.

Jane was dumbfounded. "Do you think there was a misunderstanding?"

"No, Jane, that is impossible," Elizabeth said. "There is no way to justify his behaviour. I have spent several days now, trying to make sense of it, and the only conclusion is that Wickham is a scoundrel."

"But there is such an expression of goodness in his countenance! Such an openness and gentleness in his manner."

"I know. I think he uses that to his advantage to deceive others."

Jane sat down on a turnstile, looking weary, as if she could not believe there was such wickedness in the world.

Elizabeth added, "It is not fair. Between Darcy and Wickham, one has got all the goodness and the other all the appearance of it."

Jane said, "I never thought Mr. Darcy so deficient in the appearance of it as you used to."

That was certainly true, Elizabeth thought. Jane had always championed him.

"And he has gentle hands," Jane commented.

Elizabeth frowned. "I beg your pardon?"

"Mr. Darcy. As a doctor."

"Yes, of course," Elizabeth said, remembering how she had chided him when he tried to care for her. If she could do it all again, she would be more appreciative.

Elizabeth said, "My concern now is whether I should let others know what I know about Wickham."

"Not about Miss Darcy."

"No, not that," Elizabeth agreed. "I believe Mr. Darcy told me that in confidence. And mostly likely their financial dealings as well."

Jane sighed. "And poor Wickham. It would be unkind to publish his wrongdoings before the world. Especially now when he is grieving the loss of his fiancée. Lydia thinks he truly loved Miss King. Does that not indicate that his heart has changed? Perhaps he is sorry for his past and has turned over a new leaf."

"Perhaps," Elizabeth said, although she did not believe it. "I just don't think there is anything I can say, so I had best be quiet."

"And pray," Jane said. "We can pray for comfort for him and that he is inspired to do better." She said, "And I will pray for Mr. Darcy, too."

Dear, sweet Jane, Elizabeth thought. She said, "Yes, please do."

CHAPTER THIRTEEN

Jane tried to be cheerful, but Elizabeth could tell that she was genuinely grieving the loss of Bingley. Jane had never fancied herself in love before, so her regard for him had all the warmth of a first attraction – pure and true. Elizabeth seeing her unhappiness, did not want to add to it by telling Jane what Darcy had told her about his friend – that he was unworthy of her devotion. So she said nothing.

Mrs. Bennet bemoaned the fact that Bingley was gone and that there was no talk of his coming to Netherfield again in the summer. Elizabeth was surprised that no one in Meryton knew of the Arctic journey, yet.

Kitty and Lydia cried because the militia were leaving and begged their father to take them to Brighton, but he refused.

Then Mrs. Forster invited Lydia to go with her to Brighton.

The rapture of Lydia on this occasion, her adoration of Mrs. Forster, the delight of Mrs. Bennet and the mortification of Kitty were extreme. Lydia danced about the house, exulting in her good fortune, while Kitty repined. "I cannot see why Mrs. Forster should not ask me as well as Lydia," she said, "although I am not her particular friend. I have just as much right to be asked as she has, and more too, for I am two years older."

Elizabeth tried to make Kitty see reason with no success. She also spoke to her father, expressing her concerns that Lydia should not go to Brighton. "You know how silly and reckless she is. I am afraid that with greater temptations, she will make herself and by extension, our entire family appear ridiculous."

"What – for being a flirt? I am certain Brighton is full of girls just as silly."

"It is not just silliness. She is vain, idle and completely uncontrolled. I am afraid that her unguarded and imprudent actions, combined with her ignorance may be disastrous."

"Do not make yourself uneasy," her father said. "Colonel Forster is a sensible man and will keep her out of any real mischief; and she is too poor to be an object of prey to anybody. The officers will find women better worth their notice. Let us hope, therefore, that her being there may teach her her own insignificance. Besides, there will be no peace at Longbourn if I don't let her go."

Elizabeth saw that he was determined to let her go to avoid domestic strife. She hoped that he was right and that Lydia would be safe. At least without her constant presence, there was hope that Kitty might improve.

As the days neared for Lydia's and the militia's departure, there were several social events in which Elizabeth saw Wickham in passing, but he was often surrounded by other women, and she did not want to single him out. She had expressed her condolences at the death of his fiancée and he had thanked her with a practised air. "I appreciate your kindness."

Elizabeth then overheard him telling others, "If only Miss King and I had married, then she would not have travelled with her uncle, and she would still be alive today."

Lydia said, "Do not blame yourself. You could not know that she would be attacked."

"No, but if I had been there, perhaps I could have killed her assailants." He shook his head and sighed dramatically.

Elizabeth noticed that he had let his hair grow a little longer so that he looked more poetic with one curl falling across his forehead. He was like a painting of a romantic figure, mourning the tragic loss of his fiancée. She could tell he liked the attention. She turned away in disgust. She thought it likely that Wickham grieved the loss of Miss King's dowry more than the loss of her actual person.

Later, two days before Lydia was to leave, Mrs. Bennet invited a group of officers to dine at Longbourn, including Mr. Denny and Mr. Wickham. Mr. Denny, who had often enjoyed joking with Kitty and Lydia seemed quieter than usual and thinner, as if he had not been eating well. He sat by himself, not engaging in conversation. Wickham saw Elizabeth noticing him and said quietly, "Denny has taken Miss King's death almost as hard as I have. In his own way, I think he loved her, too."

"Yes, I remember that he cared for her." Until you stole her away with your practised charm, she thought. She looked at Wickham closely, wondering how he had been put together and where his scars might be. Unlike Greenwood, his face was completely unmarked.

She found it difficult to believe that he and Darcy could be half-brothers. They were both tall with dark hair, but beyond that, there was no resemblance.

"But enough of my sorrows," Wickham said

smoothly. "I know Miss King would want me to live my life, not to spend it with constant grieving." He kissed a ring on his hand. Lydia had told her about the ring. It was gold and held a twisted knot of Miss King's hair in a miniature window. Lydia thought it was romantic. Elizabeth thought it was macabre.

Wickham said, "Let us talk of other things. I understand you recently went to Kent and spent time in Hunsford."

"Yes, I visited with Mr. and Mrs. Collins. And I met Lady Catherine de Bourgh."

"Did she meet your expectations?"

Elizabeth found it amazing that she had ever found his archness appealing. "She exceeded them," she said coolly, not giving him any encouragement to gossip. But then she decided to test him and mentioned that Colonel Fitzwilliam and Mr. Darcy had spent three weeks at Rosings. "Are you acquainted with the Colonel?"

Wickham looked surprised, displeased and alarmed, but after a moment's recollection, he managed a smile and replied that he had formerly seen the Colonel often. "He is a very gentlemanlike man. How did you like him?"

"I liked him very much."

"Did you see him often at Rosings?"

"Yes, almost every day."

"His manners are very different from his cousin's."

What a snake you are to malign Darcy, she thought, and said only, "Yes, very different. But I think Mr. Darcy improves on acquaintance."

"Indeed," said Wickham with surprise, but then he turned it to a joke. "Is it in address that he improves? Has he learned to be civil? For I dare not hope that he has improved in essentials."

"Oh, no," Elizabeth said. "In essentials, I believe he is very much what he ever was."

Wickham looked a little confused, as if not knowing whether to be pleased or alarmed by her comments.

She added, "When I said that he improved on acquaintance, I did not mean that either his mind or manners had improved, but that from knowing him better, his disposition was better understood."

Wickham's alarm now appeared in a heightened complexion and agitated look. He struggled to compose himself and said lightly, "I am glad to hear that he is wise enough to assume the appearance of what is right, even if it is not sincere." In a low voice he added, "When his father manufactured him, he must have included a brain, after all."

Elizabeth's eyes narrowed. "Come now, Mr.

Wickham," she said. "Do not tease me with your Gothic tales. I refuse to be frightened. I know Mr. Darcy's origin and yours now."

Wickham's face grew pale. "What do you know?"

"That you, rather than Mr. Darcy, are the result of - shall we say creative science and electricity?"

"Is this common knowledge?"

"No, because I believe a man should be judged by his actions, not his antecedents." Besides, it was not her story to tell, and no one would believe her if she did tell.

He bowed. "Thank you, Miss Bennet."

"I wish you well as you leave Meryton, Mr. Wickham." *And good riddance.*

* * *

Lydia danced about the house as Jane helped pack her trunks. "You may all write to me every day," she said to her sisters. "But I will be too busy going to balls and having fun to write as often!"

Kitty burst into tears and ran upstairs to her room.

"Oh, Lydia, dearest child," Mrs. Bennet said. "I will miss you terribly. But you must take every opportunity to enjoy yourself! Promise me that."

Mr. Bennet, irritated by the noise, retreated to his library and closed the door.

Elizabeth wished she had her own library as well, but since none was available, she went out to the garden to sit and read in peace.

As she left, she could hear her mother saying, "Oh, I will need to ask your father about your allowance. He must increase it. You must have spending money."

Elizabeth sighed. Although her father's income was nearly two thousand a year, there never seemed to be enough money for her mother.

She sat on a stone bench and thought about her family. With her parents as her prime example, it was difficult to imagine that conjugal felicity or domestic comfort could exist. Her father, captivated by youth and beauty, and the appearance of good humour, had married a woman with weak understanding.

Fortunately, he was a man of honour and he had not turned to drink or other vices to console himself as his affections for her had withered. He was a quiet man with a studious nature, easily amused by the folly and ignorance of others.

Elizabeth wished he had taken an effort to school or improve his wife, but he had not. He cared for her and Jane, but in many ways, he had been an absentee parent. An absentee husband.

Mrs. Philips, her mother's sister, was also silly, but she managed to work a little better with her husband, although she often deceived him, doing what she thought was best and then pretending later that he had previously given his permission.

The only good marriage Elizabeth had seen was that of her Aunt and Uncle Gardiner. Mr. Gardiner was a calm, practical man with a pleasant sense of humour. And his wife although not romantic by nature, adored him.

Elizabeth hoped someday that if she did marry, her husband could be a friend as well as a lover. She desired a man who could sympathize with her, whose eyes would reply to hers, someone gentle yet courageous, with a cultivated as well as a capacious mind, someone whose tastes were like her own.

She thought briefly of Mr. Darcy and wondered how he was faring. Did he ever think of her?

She thought of his proposal that she had dismissed so cruelly. She regretted her harsh words. She still thought they would not be happy together, he was too autocratic, and he would never have accepted her family. But in her heart, she wished him well.

She thought it amazing that he, a man of wealth and consequence, had taken the effort to study medicine. That showed him to be a man of discipline and principle.

And his care for Greenwood showed that he had a generous soul.

She thought of what Colonel Fitzwilliam had said - that he took care of his servants, his tenants and his friends. And from the conversations at Netherfield, it seemed he cared for his younger sister as well.

Where was he, she wondered. Did he have any interest in joining Bingley on his trip North?

She hoped not. She would not want him exposed to the cold and danger.

Elizabeth closed her eyes, enjoying the breeze and the warmth of the sun on her face. She heard the buzzing of the bees. She would be glad when Lydia finally left and the household was calmer. Perhaps she should take music lessons, or at least practice with Mary. She should pick a duet that they could learn together.

She sighed.

Suddenly, without warning, she felt a tightness and pain around her neck and she was pulled back, off the stone bench. She struggled, trying to claw at her assailant but from his position behind her, he had the advantage.

She tried to scream, but the sound was muffled. She could not breathe. She saw the flash of a red coat and she pulled at the tie around her throat. Her vision blurred. She kicked and threw her head back, struggling to get free, but the vice around her neck tightened and everything went dark.

CHAPTER FOURTEEN

Elizabeth woke to find herself in her own bed. Jane was sitting at her side. She put a hand to her throat which felt bruised. Her head ached. "Jane?" she asked and was alarmed by the harshness of her voice.

"Oh Lizzy, thank heavens you are awake again," Jane said. "I will get Mr. Jones."

She hurried out of the room.

Soon there was a bustle of other people in the room. Mr. Jones who ascertained that she was well enough to be questioned by Colonel Forster and the local magistrate Mr. Knowles. "Miss Bennet," Mr. Knowles said. "Did you see your assailant?"

"No," she said. "I saw a red coat, nothing more. What happened?"

"Someone tried to strangle you."

She had gathered that. "But who? And why?"

"Mr. Denny," Colonel Forster said. "He was

strangling you and Mr. Wickham came to your rescue."

"Wickham?" That did not make sense. Elizabeth said, "I don't understand." She tried to sit up, but Mr. Jones said she needed to rest and calm herself.

"Calm myself?" she demanded. "I thought I was dying."

"And you were," Mr. Knowles said flatly. "But we need to ask you what you remember."

"I was sitting, reading and then I felt something around my neck."

"So he came at you from behind?"

"Yes."

"We found the rope. From the blood on your fingers, we can tell that you struggled. Did you see the man's face?"

"No."

"Did he say anything? Did you hear anything?"

"No, I am afraid not."

"When was the last time you saw Mr. Denny?"

"At dinner last night. I may have spoken to him briefly, but I don't recall." Her head ached and it was difficult to think clearly.

"Did you notice anything a particular about him?"

"He seemed sad."

"Did he try to speak to you?"

"No."

"Thank you, very much Miss Bennet. That will be all. But if you do remember anything else, please tell us." Mr. Knowles turned to the Colonel. "I suppose we will never know the motive for it."

"Speak to Mr. Denny," Elizabeth said. "I am sure this is a misunderstanding."

"Mr. Denny is dead."

"Dead!"

"Yes, Mr. Wickham killed him to save you."

"But, Mr. Denny would never –"

"Shh, Miss Bennet," Mr. Jones interrupted. "Do not let yourself become agitated."

Elizabeth persisted. "Mr. Denny would never hurt me. Mr. Wickham might, but not Denny."

"Your friendship does you credit, Miss Bennet. But we have witnesses. Eye witnesses. And a confession."

"A confession?"

"Yes, your father heard his last words."

Tears filled Elizabeth's eyes. "None of this makes sense."

"Violence rarely does," the magistrate agreed.

"Rest now," Mr. Jones said, "And you may learn more later."

Elizabeth closed her eyes and sighed. She knew there was more she should say, but she was so tired. It was difficult to think clearly. "I will," she said weakly.

Over the next few hours, she rested and eventually she learned more. She spoke to her father who said he had looked up from the library window to see Wickham pull Denny off her and then fight him. Mr. Bennet had run outside, shouting for their servant John to assist him.

When he had arrived, Denny was on the ground, bleeding from several knife wounds. Mr. Bennet said, "He looked at me straight in the face, Lizzy, and apologized. He said, 'So sorry. I brought evil to Meryton.' Those were his last words."

"But what if his words had a different meaning?" Elizabeth said. "What if he meant he was sorry for bringing Wickham to Meryton?" The more she thought about it, the more likely she thought it that Wickham had wanted to kill her to keep his secret safe. The secret that he was not a natural man, but a combination of men created in the late Mr. Darcy's laboratory.

Her father said, "Do you not trust the man who saved your life?"

"No," Elizabeth said honestly. "I do not."

Mr. Bennet nodded. "Mr. Jones said that you might be confused after the strangulation."

"Mr. Denny and Mr. Wickham are of a similar

height. Could you have made a mistake?"

"No, Lizzy," her father said. "I saw what I saw."

Elizabeth did not know what she could do to change matters. Wickham was being hailed as a hero, when she felt in her heart that he was more likely the villain. She told the magistrate and Colonel Forster her suspicions – that Wickham had attacked her and that Denny had come to her rescue. "But why would Wickham want to harm you?" Mr. Knowles asked.

"We had a difference of opinion," she said. "I offended him."

"What about?"

Elizabeth knew they would never believe her if she told them the truth. They would think her mad if she said he was a monster. Mr. Darcy's father had done his work too well. "I said something about Mr. Darcy that he took offense to."

Colonel Forster said, "Mr. Frankenstein Darcy?"

"Yes."

"Well, we have all heard how he has treated Mr. Wickham infamously, but that is another matter, separate from this. Miss Bennet, we must follow the law, according to the facts. Mr. Denny confessed. And although it may upset you further, there is evidence that Mr. Denny was the one who killed Miss King and her uncle."

"I don't believe it."

"A bloodstained shirt was found in his belongings, as well as a gold necklace that Miss King always wore. It had been ripped from her neck."

Elizabeth shuddered. "Why would a man of intelligence save those items, unless he planned to use them to blame another?"

"Criminals are rarely intelligent," Mr. Knowles said. "And Mr. Jones believes he was suffering from moments of madness."

Elizabeth remembered what Darcy had said about Wickham, that he was angry and impulsive. Had he killed Miss King in the heat of passion and then plotted to blame Denny?

The problem was, she had no proof, only suspicions and the evidence against Denny was damning. Could she be mistaken? She knew her fears sounded like something from one of Lydia's marble backed novels.

Wickham called at Longbourn before he left town, wishing to speak to Elizabeth. Mr. Bennet thought it just and right. "We can never thank you enough for saving our daughter," he said. Mrs. Bennet escorted him upstairs.

"Mama, please," Elizabeth pleaded. "Do not leave me alone with him." She feared he might take a pillow and snuff out her life.

Mrs. Bennet tittered. "Naturally, child. I would not let you speak to a man in your bedroom alone. Come in, Mr. Wickham," she said. "I will act as chaperone."

Wickham bowed low. "Miss Bennet, I am so glad that you are not harmed. I was worried that you would not be able to speak again."

Elizabeth did not believe him. He would like nothing more than for her to be silenced.

They spoke for a few minutes, nothing but platitudes. He kissed her hand in farewell and she shivered.

He said, "I have always cared for you, Elizabeth. You were my first true friend in Meryton, and I hope you will always be my friend."

"Good bye, Mr. Wickham." *I hope I never see you again.*

Once he was gone, Mrs. Bennet scolded her for being so cold to him. "The least you could do was thank him. I think he loves you a little, and with Miss King gone, you have a chance now. Mrs. Wickham sounds very nice I think. If only he had an income of several thousand pounds a year."

"Mama, please do not pester me about it," Elizabeth said.

Later, when she learned that Lydia was still planning to leave as well, she asked her father to visit with her. He came in and sat by her bedside. Elizabeth said, "Surely you are not going to allow Lydia to go to Brighton now, after what has happened to me."

Her father disagreed. "There is evil in the world, Lizzy, but as you can see it is just as likely to happen in one's own yard as in a strange new place. I cannot build a wall around her and post guards on top. No, I think Lydia will be just as safe in Brighton as she would be in Meryton. However, I will charge Mrs. Forster not to let her go out by herself. From now on, none of my daughters will be allowed outside without companions."

This seemed excessive to Elizabeth, but she could not argue with him. Elizabeth also asked Lydia to visit her room. "Be careful, please," she said. "Do not trust Wickham."

Lydia said, "Lizzy, how mean you are. How can you say that when he saved your life!"

"He is not what he seems."

"I think being strangled has addled your brain! Wickham is a hero."

Elizabeth said, "There are rumours that he has taken advantage of young women."

Lydia made a rude noise. "I hope I am not so foolish. I would make him put a ring on my finger before I allowed any liberties."

* * *

Elizabeth recovered from her attack, but she spent the next few weeks in low spirits. She was naturally an optimistic person and had always believed that individuals could do much to improve their minds and their situations. But having someone try to kill her, reminded her that the world was full of violence and terror as well.

It seemed strange that mankind could be at once so powerful, so virtuous, and magnificent, yet so vicious and base. How could one be a scion of the evil principle and yet another almost all that could be conceived of as noble and godlike? What made the difference and what could she do to protect herself?

Whom could she trust?

She did not want to become timid and fearful, but sudden noises made her flinch and she had nightmares.

Without the militia, their parties were less varied than before and the attempted murder was a frequent topic of conversation. As Mrs. Bennet often said, "It just goes to show that no one can be trusted. Mr. Denny, who appeared to be so kind, so gentle. But the truth is, I never trusted him. There was always something sly about his eyes."

Mrs. Philips agreed. "He was too nice. That was suspicious."

Elizabeth often thought of Mr. Darcy, wondering what he would have done about Wickham, if he would have handled the situation better than she had.

She also often walked to Meryton with Kitty or Mary to purchase peppermint candies. Her mother was concerned. "Do not eat too much," Mrs. Bennet warned. "Or you will get fat."

"I will limit myself," Elizabeth promised.

Elizabeth had planned to go on a trip with her Uncle and Aunt Gardiner in June, but Mr. Gardiner's work caused it to be delayed until July. And instead of going to the Lake District, they were to visit Derbyshire. "Again?" Elizabeth asked. "But we were just there."

Mrs. Gardiner laughed. "It has been nearly eight years."

Elizabeth said quickly, "I am sorry, I should not complain. Any trip with you will be a pleasure, no matter what the destination."

The Gardiner's four children were left at Longbourn under the care of Jane, and in the morning, the Gardiners and Elizabeth set off. Elizabeth was determined to enjoy herself and to leave the melancholy of the summer behind her.

They travelled to Lambton, and Mrs. Gardiner enjoyed spending time with her prior friends. Mr.

Gardiner wanted to see Pemberley again. "I have heard that young Mr. Darcy has made some improvements."

Elizabeth was not certain she wanted to see Pemberley again, especially now when it would be a cruel reminder to her of what she had lost by refusing Mr. Darcy's hand in marriage. "Is the family in residence?" she asked. If they were, she would make up an excuse to stay at the inn.

Mr. Gardiner made enquiries and assured her that they were not.

"I am certain it will be a much quieter visit than our last one," Mrs. Gardiner said.

Elizabeth said, "I should hope so."

CHAPTER FIFTEEN

Darcy arrived at Pemberley ahead of his travelling party. He spoke to Mrs. Reynolds who told him there was a family touring the new gardens.

"Fine. I will avoid the gardens," Darcy said.

His housekeeper spoke up. "You may be interested, sir. It is the same family who was here the day you were shot, years before. The Gardiners. And a Miss Bennet."

"Miss Bennet?" He did not even take time to thank Mrs. Reynolds. He hurried to the gardens. He was filled with joy and anticipation. Elizabeth was here, at Pemberley once again.

She was standing by an arbour, dressed in white with a grey pelisse. Her hair was tucked up underneath a proper bonnet, but one curly tendril had escaped. She looked more thin than he remembered. "Elizabeth!" he cried, then corrected himself. He must act with decorum, even when he wanted to rush to her and welcome her with open arms. "Miss Bennet, forgive me."

She looked at him, surprised, but he could not read her expression well enough to know if she was pleased to see him. "There is nothing to forgive," she said politely.

Did she still hate him? It was impossible to tell. He said, "How good it is to see you."

She looked embarrassed. "I did not –" She stopped. "We had heard that you were not in residence or we would never have intruded upon your privacy."

"No," he said quickly. "You would never be an inconvenience. I am happy to see you again. Are you well?"

"Yes, sir."

Surely it was not merely politeness that made her smile. He asked, "And your family?"

"As far as I know, they are all well. I am travelling with my aunt and uncle."

He glanced over at the middle aged couple who were watching their interaction with interest. "Please do me the honour of introducing me to your family," he said.

"You don't mind?" she asked.

"No, certainly not. I would be glad to meet any member of your family." He looked into her eyes as he spoke and hoped that she would realize that he had taken her prior words to heart.

He had been proud before, thinking himself above her and her family. He hoped now to show her that he had changed.

Elizabeth performed the introduction. He was pleased to see that her aunt and uncle were intelligent people of taste. They were worlds above Mrs. Bennet, but at that moment, he would have been thrilled to speak to that woman as well if it would make Elizabeth happy. They spoke for several minutes. Darcy referred to the shooting accident years ago and expressed his gratitude for Elizabeth. "Her quick thinking made all the difference."

Mr. and Mrs. Gardiner were pleased.

Darcy said, "And you, sir, I believe you helped as well?"

"Not at all. Mostly I tried to stay out of the way. But I did say some prayers for your recovery."

"They were much appreciated, thank you."

The conversation then continued in a lighter vein. Mr. Gardiner mentioned that he liked to fish and Darcy invited him to come and obtain some rod and tackle. "How long are you planning to stay in the area?" he asked. "We could arrange a time. Sometime this week perhaps?"

Mr. Gardiner looked at his wife who smiled her approval. "I would enjoy that, yes."

"But first, would you like some refreshment? Tea? Lemonade?"

The Gardiners declined, but he pressed further and Mrs. Gardiner admitted that she would like some lemonade. Darcy walked with them back to the house and he spoke with a footman who brought Mrs. Reynolds.

Within half an hour, they were all seated outside with lemonade and sandwiches. Darcy walked with Elizabeth a little far off, so he could show her a view of the maze he had recently designed. "How clever," she said. "When I was younger, I always wanted to visit a garden maze."

"So did Georgiana. She showed me pictures in a book."

"You are a kind brother."

But not as good as he would wish. He said, "It is a work in progress, but within a year or two, it will be finished. Would you like to see a closer view?" he asked.

"I would."

He asked the Gardiners if they would like to join them, but they, glancing at each other, smiled and declined. Darcy decided that if they would let him spend time with Elizabeth alone, they were ideal relations. Mrs. Gardiner asked Elizabeth if she felt up to it.

"Yes, aunt, thank you. I am fine."

"Very well then. We will watch you from here."

Elizabeth nodded.

Darcy offered his arm, she took it, and together they walked down a slight hill to the new garden maze. "Your aunt was concerned. Have you been ill? I thought you said you were well."

"Yes, but she is protective." Elizabeth looked away for a moment, then said quietly, "Perhaps you heard about it or read it in the newspapers. Two months ago, someone tried to strangle me."

To Darcy, it was like a blow to his heart. "Who? Where? Are you all right now?"

"Yes, yes, I am fine," she assured him. "I was at home, at Longbourn."

"But how?"

"I was sitting in a garden. Mr. Denny was blamed, but I believe that it was Wickham."

"Wickham?"

She explained briefly. "I do not know all the details for I was unconscious. I think Wickham attacked me and Denny fought him, but by the time I had revived, Denny was dead and Wickham claimed he had rescued me."

"Was nothing done?"

"No. There was nothing I more I could do. No one believed me, and the evidence was against me. I did not share your letter because I felt that with the prejudice against Denny and for Wickham, that it would do no good."

He nodded. "You are right. And whether or not he was a re-creation of my father would be irrelevant as to his guilt. Wickham has an impulsive angry temper. He will lash out then later repent of it. And he is a master liar. But I did not think him capable of murder."

"I believe he wanted to kill me because I told him that I knew he had been reanimated."

"I should not have told you. I put you at risk."

"No," she said quickly. "It was my mistake to tell him. I sleep poorly now at night, fearful that I might be murdered like Miss King."

Darcy frowned, confused at the reference.

"Mr. Wickham's fiancée. She and her uncle were murdered a few weeks earlier."

"And Wickham was not suspect?"

"No, again there was evidence against Denny."

Darcy fought back a wave of anger. "This is outrageous. I wish I could take care of you. Protect you."

At this, Elizabeth blushed and looked away.

He had said too much. "Forgive me," Darcy said quickly. "I presume too much, and your aunt and uncle will think I have abducted you." He walked with her back up the hill, wishing he could keep her safe at Pemberley. It frightened him to his very soul that she could have died.

Darcy spoke with her relations. After a few minutes he said, "The rest of my party are due to arrive tomorrow. They include my younger sister Georgiana whom I would like to introduce to you, and those who already claim an acquaintance: Mr. Bingley, his sister Miss Bingley and the Hursts. Would you please do me the honour of dining with us the evening after that?"

Mr. Gardiner said they had not been planning to stay so long in Lambton, but they would be happy to extend their visit.

Darcy said, "Excellent. I look forward to it."

* * *

On the ride back to Lambton, Mr. Gardiner praised Darcy. "I will admit I am surprised. Mr. Darcy is perfectly well behaved, polite and unassuming."

"Definitely not what we were expecting," Mrs. Gardiner agreed. "He was more than civil. He was really attentive, but some of that may have been his gratitude for you, Lizzy. Why did you tell us before that he was so disagreeable?"

Elizabeth blushed, wishing that she had never spoken ill of him to her family. "His manners in Hertfordshire were not so open. I got to know him a little better when I was in Kent, but I agree, I have never seen him so agreeable as he was today."

Mr. Gardiner said, "Great men can be whimsical in their civilities. Should I take him at his word about fishing, or do you think he will change his mind and later warn me off his grounds?"

"Oh no," Elizabeth said quickly. "Mr. Darcy is a man of his word. I believe he will honour both his invitations – to fish and to have us dine with him."

Mrs. Gardiner nodded. "Very good. I like him. There is something of dignity in his countenance but he is not ill natured."

"No," Elizabeth agreed. She thought of his smile when he first saw her. He seemed so different from the man he had been before. Never, even in the company of his friends at Netherfield had she seen him so desirous to please, so free from self-consequence or unbending reserve.

Her aunt said, "I am surprised, though, to think him capable of treating Wickham so cruelly."

Elizabeth said, "I think we should take Wickham's version of the events with a pinch of salt. My understanding is that Mr. Darcy did not leave him destitute."

"Indeed," Mrs. Gardiner said, but did not press her for the source of that information. "I am glad to hear it."

Two days later, they dined at Pemberley. In the intervening time, Elizabeth had opportunity to examine her own feelings. She no longer hated Mr. Darcy. She could not hate him after his letter, even though she had held onto a level of dislike out of principle. But now, after all that had happened with Wickham and seeing Darcy at Pemberley, her heart and mind were in turmoil.

She was amazed that he could treat her kindly after her rejection. She was not so vain as to think that he would address her again, but the fact that he could treat her and her family members with respect, that he actively sought their regard, pleased her. It showed that he was not resentful, that he had a noble, generous disposition.

On the day of the dinner, Mr. Gardiner spent several hours fishing with Mr. Darcy, and returned to dress for the evening's activities. Elizabeth overheard Mrs. Gardiner asking him about his sport, and Elizabeth left the room so she would not pester him with her own questions. *How was Mr. Darcy? Was he well? Did he ask about me?*

Elizabeth took extra care to dress for dinner, but her hair was uncooperative. If she brushed it, it would explode into a tangled halo, so she tied up what she could with ribbons. Mrs. Gardiner when she saw her, tsked her tongue and added a few hairpins. "Smile, Lizzy," she said. "And no one will notice your hair."

Elizabeth was anxious to meet Georgiana. She had heard so much about her from Miss Bingley, Wickham, Lady Catherine and Darcy himself, she was finally going to see her for herself.

Georgiana was tall and on a larger scale than Elizabeth herself, and although she was only sixteen, her figure was formed and her appearance womanly and graceful. There was sense and good humour in her face, and her manners gentle. She was shy, though, and sometimes when not being addressed, when her features were at rest, there was a slight frown to her eyebrows, similar to her brother's.

Upon noticing this, Elizabeth looked at Mr. Darcy more closely, analysing his features. She determined that he had not always been scowling at her in the past, it was merely a reflection of his own pensive thoughts and the angle of his brows.

He saw her looking at him and raised one of those eyebrows in question. She smiled at him, but did not comment. She was rewarded by a hint of frown. He was thinking about her.

Mrs. Gardiner, noticing her elation, glanced meaningfully at her own husband.

It was all Elizabeth could do to keep from laughing with joy.

Miss Bingley, still haughty, still superior, addressed her when Georgiana was playing a song on the pianoforte. "Miss Eliza," she said, "How sad you must have been to have the militia leave Meryton."

"No, actually, after my experience, I was glad to see them go."

"Oh, that's right. Your name was in the newspapers. Shocking."

"Which do you find more shocking – that I was nearly killed or that my name was in the newspapers?"

Miss Bingley sniffed. "A young lady does not want her name bandied about by the press."

"Then I will endeavour not to be a victim again. Or if I am, perhaps I should hope that I will be murdered so I do not have to live through the shame."

Miss Bingley said quickly, "Forgive me. I did not mean to cause you distress."

"No?"

"And how stunned we were to learn that Wickham was your hero. That was convenient, considering that he had been a favourite of yours."

Georgiana paled and her fingers faltered. Elizabeth walked over to the pianoforte to help her turn pages.

Darcy, watching this situation with concern, interjected. "This is hardly a conversation suitable for this evening," he said coolly.

Elizabeth sent him a thankful glance and he responded with a smile.

Later in the evening, Elizabeth spoke with Mr. Bingley. She had wondered how she would feel when she saw him again, if loyalty to her sister would make her dislike him. But she could not. He was the same friendly gentleman he had been before, although possibly a little quieter. She said to him, "I am glad to see you again. I had heard that you were going to the Arctic on a geographic expedition."

"I was," Bingley said. "But I changed my mind."

Mercurial, Elizabeth thought. Just as Darcy had warned. Perhaps it was best that he no longer cared for Jane.

Bingley said, "Tell me about your family. Are they all well? Are they all at home?'

"Yes, we are all well. One of my sisters, Lydia, is not at home. She has gone to Brighton with a friend."

"But your oldest sister is at home."

"Yes." Could he not even say Jane's name?

He smiled nervously. "I am planning to return to Netherfield shortly. I hope to see all of your family soon."

"Except for Lydia," she reminded.

"Yes, except for Lydia," he said and smiled.

Elizabeth walked away, slightly annoyed. From his hints, it appeared that Bingley might still care for her sister. But she would not tell Jane that she had met him again, for there was no guarantee that he would return to Netherfield. He might change his mind again.

* * *

After his guests left, Darcy returned to the salon. Miss Bingley said, "How very ill Eliza Bennet looked this evening. I never in my life saw anyone so much altered as she is since the winter. She is grown so brown and coarse! Louisa and I were agreeing that we should not have known her again."

At that moment, Darcy was regretting ever inviting Bingley or his family to Pemberley. Caroline Bingley was a spiteful cat, but he must say something, so he replied coolly, "I did not perceive any alteration, other than her being a little tan, which is to be expected after travelling in the summer."

"For my own part," Miss Bingley continued. "I must confess I never could see any beauty in her. Her face is too thin; her complexion has no brilliancy; and her features are not at all handsome. Her nose lacks distinction, her teeth are only tolerable, and her eyes, which have sometimes been called fine, have a sharp shrewish look."

Mrs. Hurst nodded her approval. "And her poor hair! I almost laughed out loud when I saw it tonight. Like a haystack!"

Darcy had thought the arrangement charming. The pile of dark curls had made his fingers itch to remove the ribbons and watch her hair fall to her shoulders.

Bingley looked uncomfortable at his sister's tirade and Georgiana frowned, but Miss Bingley continued. "I remember, when we first knew her, how amazed we all were to find that she was a reputed beauty. I particularly recollect your saying one night, after they had been dining at Netherfield, 'She a beauty – I should as soon call her mother a wit.' But afterwards she seemed to improve upon you, and I believe you thought her rather pretty at one time."

Darcy could contain himself no longer. "Yes, but that was only when I first knew her, for it is many months since I have considered her as one of the handsomest women of my acquaintance."

For a moment, Miss Bingley's mouth gaped open like a fish, but then she turned to Georgiana to talk to her.

Darcy walked across the room to stare at the fireplace. The sooner the Bingleys left Pemberley, the better.

Eventually the women retired for bed and he was alone with Bingley. Darcy yawned. It had been a long day. He liked Mr. Gardiner and had enjoyed the day's fishing, but that, and arranging for the dinner had taken its toll. And then to have Miss Bingley upset Georgiana by mentioning Wickham. He had worried for a moment that she might burst into tears. But thank goodness for Elizabeth's kindness, disaster had been avoided.

Bingley said, "Do you want to stay up longer or are you going to bed?"

"To bed, I think," Darcy said. "But first, a question for you."

Bingley looked at him expectantly.

"Are you considering going back to Netherfield?"

Bingley nodded. "It is my house, after all. It is foolish to rent the place and never live there."

"But why?" Darcy persisted.

"I still think of her."

Neither of them needed to say her name. Darcy said only, "Don't pursue her unless you can be constant."

Bingley sighed. "It is different this time. I truly believe I love her."

Darcy said, "I hope you do. Good night."

He walked upstairs to the master bedroom. On the way, he knocked on Greenwood's door. The man grunted and he opened the door.

He saw Greenwood sitting up in bed reading a book. He wore a nightshirt and cap. There was a candle beside him on the table, and the uneven light flickered over his heavy, scarred features.

"You need more light," Darcy said. "You will ruin your eyes."

Greenwood rolled his eyes. He then made a questioning noise and brought his fist to his chest. He tapped twice over his heart and pointed at Darcy.

Darcy frowned. "I don't understand."

Greenwood smiled and made the curving motion that had meant Elizabeth, then struck his chest again and pointed.

Darcy smiled. Greenwood was very observant. He knew that Elizabeth was no longer just a pretty woman. She was his own heart now. "Yes, I spoke with her. It was very nice."

Greenwood touched his ring finger and raised his eyebrows.

"Not yet," Darcy said and laughed as he closed the door. He had never realized what a romantic Greenwood was.

Once in his room, he also prepared for bed. He could not help but think of Elizabeth and wonder if she liked him. Her smiles had warmed his heart, but was it too soon to ask her to marry him?

This time, he would do a better job.

And if he did ask her, he wanted to have a ring. He opened the adjoining door to his mother's bedroom. Her belongings were still there. The room had been left unchanged since his mother's death, but Mrs. Reynolds had made certain it was cleaned regularly.

As he looked about the room, he thought of her death and how greatly he still missed her. She had died while he was recovering from his abdominal surgery. "A fever," his father had said at the time. He had been too upset to say anything more.

Darcy understood his pain. There were no words to relieve the feelings of those whose dearest ties are rent by the irreparable evil of death. Death was a void that presented itself to the very soul. It took so long to accept the fact that she whom they saw every day and whose every existence appeared a part of their own could have departed forever. He did not know how his father endured the loss – the brightness of his beloved's eye had been extinguished and the sound of her voice so familiar and dear had been hushed, never more to be heard.

But as time passed, outward grief became an indulgence. His father resumed his duties, but sometimes when he looked at Darcy or Georgiana, Darcy sensed he was fearful that they, too, might be untimely snatched from his grasp.

After his father died, Darcy had asked Mrs. Reynolds about his mother's death. "It was sudden," she said. "Everyone was concerned about you and she just slipped away in her sleep. I think your accident may have broken her heart."

Darcy often wished he could have spoken to her one last time before she died.

He opened a closet door and touched one of her gowns, a blue striped dress he remembered. He wondered what she would have thought of Elizabeth. Would she have welcomed her into her home?

He walked over to her jewellery chest, but it was locked.

He looked through her desk to see if he could find a key. Eventually he did find a key, but it was underneath a bound journal.

He did not know that his mother had written a diary, other than the day book for the house that outlined her household duties which he had seen years before. He set his candle down on the desk top and flipped through the pages, happy to see her familiar handwriting.

He turned towards the end of the entries, wanting to read her last words. Inside the journal was a folded letter, addressed to his mother. He opened the letter and read a short note written from a young Jane Bennet telling his mother that he had asked her to tell his parents that he loved them. He smiled, grateful at least that his mother had received the message. He folded the letter back up and read the last entry which was short. The handwriting was uneven.

My son is dead. The joy of my life taken by a villain's bullet. Shot dead on one of Pemberley's walks.

He is dead and should be buried, but my husband wants to save him, just as he saved young Wickham.

I begged of him, pleaded with him not to do it, but I recognize the madness in his eyes. He will not give up Frankenstein.

I told him I refused to let him buy corpses. "You will not put some stranger's guts in my son! If you must, you may take some of my own intestines."

My husband did not agree, but I was determined. I pray to God that the surgeries go well.

Under this, there were two lines dated a few days later in his father's handwriting.

Both surgeries a success and Frankenstein was re-animated. But Lady Anne contracted a fever and died. May God have mercy on my soul. GD

CHAPTER SIXTEEN

Darcy shrank back and sat on his mother's bed. So many things made sense now – his poor digestion, his father's grief and guilt, even the connection he felt to Greenwood.

His sainted mother, dead at her husband's hands.

A risky surgery that should never have been performed.

Was he a monster now, like Greenwood and Wickham?

He thought of Elizabeth and how he would tell her and wondered how she would react. She had always treated Greenwood with respect, but the thought of marrying a man who had been brought back to life was another matter. And he was not certain she would even consider marrying him. Would she be like his own mother, horrified by his father's actions?

Darcy flipped through more of his mother's diary.

He read what she said about Wickham's re-animation. She had been furious with his father for breaking his promise not to conduct such experiments and for nearly a year they had been estranged. But he noticed there was no hint in the diary that Wickham was his father's son. At least his mother had been spared that knowledge.

Darcy decided he would go to Lambton in the morning and offer to take Elizabeth for a ride in his curricle so they could talk before she came to visit Georgiana that afternoon.

When he arrived at the inn, a servant took him to a sitting room, announcing his presence.

But upon his entrance he saw Elizabeth in an agitated state, saying, "My uncle. Where is my uncle?" Belatedly she recognized him and said, "I beg your pardon, but I must leave you. I must find Mr. Gardiner this moment, on business that cannot be delayed. I have not an instant to lose."

"Good God! What is the matter?" he cried with more feeling than politeness, then recollected himself. "I will not detain you a minute, but let me, or let the servant go after Mr. and Mrs. Gardiner. You are not well enough. You cannot go yourself."

Elizabeth hesitated, but she let him walk her to a chair to sit down. "Yes, you are right."

Darcy called the servant back and Elizabeth gave them the Gardiners' direction and a charge to find them.

Darcy said, "You are ill. Is there something I can do to help? A glass of wine perhaps?"

Elizabeth shook her head. "No, thank you. There is nothing the matter with me. I am merely distressed by news I have just received from Longbourn."

At this, she burst into tears and for a few moments could not speak another word. Darcy paced the room, imagining the worst. Had Mr. Bennet died? Or someone else in her family? "I wish there was something I could do to relieve your pain."

She said finally, "I have just had a letter from Jane with such dreadful news. It cannot be concealed for long. Lydia – poor stupid Lydia – has eloped with Wickham."

Darcy drew his breath in sharply.

"They are gone off together from Brighton. You know him too well to doubt the rest. She has no money, no connections, nothing that could tempt him to marry her."

She was right. Wickham would never marry a girl with Lydia's meagre dowry.

"When I consider," she added in a more agitated voice. "that I might have prevented it. I who knew what he was. If I could have explained it completely to my own family, it might have stopped her. I don't think she would care about his dishonest money dealings, but she might have been disgusted to know that he was not a whole man. But it is all too late."

Darcy said, "I am grieved, indeed, shocked. But is it certain, absolutely certain?"

"Yes, they left Brighton together on Sunday night and were traced almost to London, but not beyond; they are certainly not gone to Scotland."

Which meant he had no plans to marry her over the anvil. "And what has been done to recover her?"

"My father is gone to London and Jane has written to beg my uncle's immediate assistance. And we shall be off, I hope in half an hour. But I know nothing can be done. How is he to be discovered? I have not the smallest hope. For all I know, he will kill her as he tried to kill me."

Darcy did not know what to say, for he agreed with her. Lydia had put herself in grave danger – her reputation as well as her person.

Elizabeth turned on him. She said angrily, "It is all your father's fault. If he had just let Wickham die, this would not have happened."

Darcy stepped back as if she had struck him.

She cried, "This is what comes from tampering with

the divine powers of life – more evil let loose upon the world. Mary King dead. Denny dead. And now my poor sister in his wicked grasp. Would that Wickham had never come to Meryton."

Darcy put his hand on her shoulder to comfort her and she wept again. Elizabeth said, "I should have said something different, done something different. But no one would have believed me."

With every tear, he felt as if she was cutting out his heart, for he knew she was right. Wickham was his responsibility, too. He said, "Forgive me. No doubt you have long been desiring my absence. Would to heaven that I could do something to ease your concern and distress. But I will not torment you with vain hopes. Instead, I will take my leave. This unfortunate affair will, I fear, prevent a ride at Pemberley today and my sister's having the pleasure of seeing you."

Elizabeth sniffed, trying to compose herself. "Thank you. Be so kind as to thank Miss Darcy for her invitation. Conceal the unhappy truth as long as it is possible. I know it cannot be long."

"I will keep your secrets," he promised. "And I hope that ultimately all will be well." He took her hand and kissed it. "Farewell, Miss Bennet. God bless you and your unfortunate sister. Please give my compliments to your aunt and uncle." He bowed and left the room quickly.

He would leave for London within an hour.

* * *

When Mr. Gardiner heard the news about Lydia, he was not as concerned as Elizabeth or Mrs. Gardiner. "I cannot believe that a young man as intelligent as Wickham would design against a young woman who was staying with his own colonel. It would be madness, a violation of decency, honour, and his own interest."

Elizabeth thought of the tie as it had tightened around her neck. One of the young men was mad – whether Wickham or Denny, she would never know. "I think Wickham capable of anything, if he thought he would not be caught."

They travelled quickly to Longbourn, taking only two days. When they arrived, Mrs. Bennet was inconsolable. "To think of our Wickham, who had been so good to Lizzy, secretly a villain! Poor Lydia. It is all the Forsters' fault, for if they had watched over Lydia, she would never have run away. And brother, you must go to London quickly and find Mr. Bennet, and help him find Wickham and make him marry her."

"I will do what I can," Mr. Gardiner promised.

Elizabeth spoke with Jane. "Who knows of our trials?"

"All of Meryton, most likely. When we first received the express, Mama was intemperate in her speech."

Elizabeth sighed. It was as she had feared. What gossip the Bennets had provided: one daughter nearly killed, another running off with a scoundrel.

"I cannot think Wickham so very bad," Jane said. "He knows Lydia does not have a large dowry. So he must truly care for her."

Jane was too good. "And what of Miss King? Did he care for her as well?"

"Perhaps Lydia is consoling him."

Elizabeth did not want to consider what that might involve. "Oh, Jane," she said wearily. "What are we to do?"

"Wait," Jane said. "Wait and pray for the best. It is all we can do."

The Gardiners returned to London and within two days there was a letter from Mr. Bennet. Mr. Gardiner had joined him, but they were unable to find Wickham.

Mrs. Bennet worried that if they did find him, that Mr. Bennet would challenge Wickham to a duel. "Then he will kill your father, and the Collinses will throw us out!" she wailed.

Elizabeth tried to be patient with her mother, but if the truth were known, she felt like crying as well.

She doubted she would ever see Darcy again. And if she did, he would not welcome her into his home. How could he, when Lydia's disgrace would affect her entire family? He would not want his sister to be acquainted with the Bennets. He already thought her family vulgar and unprincipled. Lydia's actions had merely proven him correct.

And she had not been at her best, either – crying and blaming his father, acting like a shrew.

No wonder Darcy had left the inn so quickly, eager to get away from her.

There was no escaping the truth. Elizabeth had lost Mr. Darcy, just when she was beginning to think she might want him for the rest of her life.

* * *

Once in London, Darcy hired a Bow Street Runner and spoke to Mrs. Younge. After bribes and threats, he finally obtained Wickham's address.

The landlady, a small heavyset woman with a dirty cap and apron, escorted Darcy upstairs to a dark, narrow room. "I didn't know they weren't married," she said defensively.

She knocked on the door and Darcy opened it

without waiting for Wickham's permission.

The room was a disaster with dirty linens and food and dishes on the floor. He saw Lydia lying on the bed, one arm hanging down so that her hand rested on the floor. "Miss Bennet," he called out to wake her, as he hurried to her side.

But she would never waken, for she was dead, several hours' dead from the look of it. Darcy felt oddly detached, as if he were observing a corpse at medical school. He had known for years that his half-brother was a villain, but here was final proof that he was a murderer as well. Darcy had no more doubts, no more hope that Wickham could somehow be redeemed.

The landlady started crying. "Oh, the poor child. I never knew. I swear I never knew."

"Silence!" Darcy said sharply. With clinical expertise, he carefully examined the body. Wickham had strangled Lydia first, then stabbed a knife into her heart.

CHAPTER SEVENTEEN

Mr. Bennet stayed in London for three weeks, but as the search for Wickham and Lydia continued with no success, he returned to Longbourn. Mr. Gardiner planned to extend the search efforts, but Elizabeth thought they would fail. London was too large. A man determined to be hidden would stay hidden.

When Mr. Bennet arrived, he said little. Jane expressed concern for his health and the strain he had been through.

"Say nothing of that," he said sharply. "Who should suffer but myself? It has been my own doing, and I ought to feel it."

Elizabeth said, "You must not be too severe upon yourself."

"No, Lizzy," he said. "Let me once in my life feel how much I have been to blame. I am not afraid of being overpowered by the impression. It will pass away soon enough."

"Do you suppose them to be in London?"

"Yes, where else can they be so well concealed?"

"Lydia always wanted to go to London," Kitty added.

"She is happy, then," said her father, dryly. "And her residence there will probably be of some duration." He turned to Elizabeth. "I bear you no ill will for being justified in your advice to me last May, which considering the past events, shows some greatness of mind."

Jane would not give up hope. "Perhaps they have gone to Scotland after all."

"You think that, Jane, if it gives you hope," Mr. Bennet said.

Mary interrupted them, coming to fetch her mother's tea.

"Does your mother still stay in her room, in her dressing gown?" Mr. Bennet asked.

"Yes, sir."

He nodded. "Ah, it gives such elegance to misfortune. Perhaps I will do the same. I will sit in my library in my night cap and powdering gown and give as much trouble as I can. Or perhaps I may defer it, until Kitty runs away."

"I am not going to run away," Kitty said fretfully. "If I should ever go to Brighton, I would behave better than Lydia."

"You go to Brighton! No, not for fifty pounds! No, Kitty, I have at last learnt to be cautious, and you will feel the effects of it. No officer is ever to enter my house again, nor even to pass through the village. Balls will be absolutely prohibited, unless you stand up with one of your sisters. And you are never to stir out of doors, till you can prove that you have spent ten minutes of every day in a rational manner."

Kitty, who took these threats in a serious light, began to cry.

"There, there, child," he said more kindly. "Do not make yourself unhappy. If you are a good girl for the next ten years, I will take you to a review at the end of them."

* * *

Ten days after Mr. Bennet's return, as Jane and Elizabeth were walking together in the gardens behind the house, they saw the housekeeper coming towards them. "I beg your pardon, madam, for interrupting you, but I was in hopes you might have got some good news from Town, so I took the liberty of coming to ask."

"What do you mean? We have heard nothing from Town."

Mrs. Hill was astonished. "There was an express come for the master half an hour earlier."

Elizabeth ran back to the house with Jane, who was not in the habit of running, lagging behind. They found their father outside, walking towards a small wood on one side of the paddock.

"Oh Papa, what news?" Elizabeth cried. "Have you heard from my uncle?"

"Yes. I have had a letter from him by express."

"Well, and what news does it bring? Good or bad?"

"What is there of good to be expected?" he said, taking the letter from his pocket. "But perhaps you would like to read it."

Elizabeth impatiently caught his hand and took the letter. She unfolded it with shaking hands.

"Read it aloud," said her father.

My dear Brother —

At last I am able to send you some tidings of my niece, and such as, upon the whole, will give you peace.

Lydia has been found. Wickham abandoned her. We have not been able to trace him. Lydia, understandably, is not in good health and has been recovering at a private hospital. The doctors believe that she will be able to travel within a month or two.

When she is better, I will arrange her travel back to Longbourn. There is no need for your coming to Town again, but I believe the patient would appreciate some letters from you and her family. If you send them to me, I will see that she receives them.

I will also take care of her expenses.

In the meantime, I believe it would be best to put out the word that she was ill at Brighton and travelled here for medical treatment. Perhaps that will stem the gossip.

I shall write again as I learn more,

Yours, etc.

"Oh, thank heavens," Elizabeth said. "She is alive."

"Poor Lydia," Jane said. "How she must be suffering."

"And may still suffer," Mr. Bennet said. "As we may all suffer."

They both looked at him.

"I fear Lydia may be with child."

Jane gasped. "Surely not!"

Mr. Bennet shook his head. "Why else would she need to stay away so long? I think your uncle is not telling us the entire truth. He will extend her stay for a year, and then Lydia will return as if nothing had happened."

"And the child?"

"Most likely placed in another home, with funds for the child's support."

"How much would that be?"

"Several thousand, possibly more. Your uncle is a generous, good man, but I fear that he will distress himself. I don't know how I will repay him."

"Should Mama know?" Jane asked.

"No," Mr. Bennet said firmly. "She would want to keep the grandchild. And if she did, none of you would find husbands."

"I don't think I will ever marry," Elizabeth said.

* * *

Upon learning that Lydia had been found, Mrs. Bennet chose to leave her bedroom and resume her social obligations. She promoted the story that Lydia had been ill, but in private she talked often of Wickham. "I don't know why your uncle does not pursue him further. I still think he should be made to marry Lydia."

Elizabeth tried to talk wisdom to her but with no success. Elizabeth spent many hours walking outside in the last summer days. The weather was fine, and the skies cloudless. Rather than count her sorrows, Elizabeth was determined to enjoy the beautiful flowers and verdure. Her senses were gratified and refreshed by a thousand scents of delight and a thousand sights of beauty.

Now that Lydia was out of danger, she wished she had not told Darcy about her elopement. She did not think he would spread the gossip, but she wished he did not have to think so poorly of her and her family.

In September, Mrs. Philips brought the news that Mr. Bingley was returning to Netherfield. Mrs. Bennet out of loyalty to Jane, spoke coldly. "Why should we care, either way, what Mr. Bingley does? He is nothing to us, you know, and I am sure I never want to see him again after the way he slighted poor Jane."

Jane looked away, embarrassed and later spoke to Elizabeth. "I saw how you looked at me, Lizzy. I know I looked distressed, but I am not, I was merely confused, knowing that everyone would be looking at me, expecting a reaction."

"It is hard," Elizabeth said, "That the poor man cannot come to a house, which he has legally hired, without raising all this speculation."

"I thoroughly agree," Jane said.

When Mr. Bingley finally arrived, he called on the Bennet family. Mrs. Bennet told him about the Collinses' marriage and Lydia's recent illness and added that she should be home soon. Mr. Bingley spoke to Elizabeth, reminding her that he had been happy to see her at Pemberley, even though her visit to Derbyshire had been cut short."

"Yes, it was good to see you and your sisters. Are they travelling with you?'

"No, I came alone to hunt."

"I am surprised you did not bring your friend Mr. Darcy," she said lightly.

He looked at her. "He is very busy with his new hospital in London."

"So he has started that."

"Yes."

"Then I am happy for him. He seems a man who is best kept occupied."

Bingley smiled. "Yes. There is nothing worse than Darcy on a Sunday evening when he has nothing to do."

Elizabeth smiled, but she thought that she would not mind seeing him again, even on a Sunday.

Over the next two weeks, they saw Bingley several times and then one morning, he requested an audience with Mr. Bennet.

Elizabeth glanced at Jane, who looked away and blushed.

"When did this happen?" Elizabeth teased.

"At Mrs. Cole's, when everyone was playing cards,"

Jane said quietly.

"And you did not tell me?"

Jane shook her head. "I could not, not until I knew for certain."

Jane must have her own doubts, Elizabeth thought and could not blame her. Personally, she would not believe that Bingley would marry her until the ring was on her finger.

But within a few minutes, Bingley and Mr. Bennet returned with the happy announcement. Bingley stayed for dinner and the mood was joyful, except for one tearful comment from Mrs. Bennet, "If only Lydia were here as well."

Later, when Bingley had left, Mr. Bennet said, "Jane, I congratulate you. You will be a very happy woman."

"I believe I will, sir."

"I have no doubt of your doing well together. Your tempers are alike. You are each of you so complying that nothing will ever be resolved on; so easy, that every servant will cheat you and so generous, that you will always exceed your income."

"Exceed their income! My dear Mr. Bennet," cried Mrs. Bennet. "What are you talking of? Why, he has four or five thousand a year, and very likely more." She embraced her oldest daughter. "Oh my dear, dear Jane, I am so happy. I knew how it would be. I was sure you could not be so beautiful for nothing. Oh, he is the handsomest young man that ever was seen!"

That night, Jane spoke to Elizabeth privately in her room. "So you really like him?" Elizabeth teased.

"Oh, Lizzy," Jane said. "Sometimes I think it is too much. I must be the happiest creature in the world. I do not deserve it."

"Well, if you don't deserve happiness, I don't know who would," Elizabeth said dryly.

Jane said, "I wish I could see you as happy. If there were but such another man for you."

Elizabeth remembered Mr. Darcy's proposal, but she had refused him. She said, "If you were to give me forty such men, I never could be so happy as you. Until I have your disposition, your goodness, I can never have your happiness." She laughed. "But perhaps, with luck, I may meet with another Mr. Collins."

* * *

Mrs. Bennet thought that with Jane's engagement, she was the happiest woman in Hertfordshire, but her happiness was increased when Mr. Gardiner appeared one evening with Lydia.

Mrs. Bennet squealed. "My dearest girl! Oh you are home at last, but so thin. Lydia, we shall have to fatten you up!"

Lydia greeted everyone with smiles. "It is good to be home. Father, Mama, thank you for taking me back. And I apologize most sincerely for the heartache I have caused."

Elizabeth glanced at Jane. She could not remember Lydia ever apologizing before.

Over the next few days, Elizabeth observed her. Lydia seemed quieter, calmer. One day she sat with Jane and Elizabeth in the garden rather than joining Kitty and Mary in a walk to Meryton. Elizabeth was surprised she did not want to join them. "Are you feeling poorly?"

"No," Lydia said. "I am having my courses, but that is of no matter. I would rather spend the time with you. There is nothing in Meryton to excite my interest."

Elizabeth glanced at Jane, who nodded, equally surprised. But at least they now knew Lydia was not pregnant.

"Do you feel that you have recovered now?" Jane asked.

"Yes."

"I know you haven't told Mama the details, which is probably wise," Elizabeth said. "But I cannot help but wonder how it all came about, that you are safe at home. The last thing we heard was that you had eloped with Wickham."

Lydia blushed. "Yes, in my foolishness, I thought his proposal romantic."

"You don't need to give us details," Jane assured her.

"No, I want to," Lydia said. "At least what I can share." She reached out for Elizabeth's hand. "And you were right to warn me about Wickham. He tried to strangle me."

Jane gasped and Elizabeth brought her hand up to her throat, remembering her attack. "How did you get free?'

"I don't know, but when I woke at Pemberley, I -"

"Pemberley? I thought you were in London."

"Gracious me! I ought not to have said a word about it. I promised Mr. Darcy and Uncle Gardiner so faithfully. It is such a secret."

"If it was to be a secret," said Jane. "Say not another word on the subject. You may depend on my seeking no further."

"Oh, certainly," said Elizabeth agreed, although she was burning with curiosity. "We will ask you no more questions."

"Thank you," said Lydia, "For if you did, I should certainly tell you all, and then Mr. Darcy would be angry." There was a hint of the old Lydia in her melodramatics.

Elizabeth wrote to her aunt that evening. "You may readily comprehend what my curiosity must be on this matter – how he came to be involved with her recovery. Pray write instantly, and let me understand it - unless it is, to remain in secrecy."

Elizabeth had the satisfaction of receiving an answer to her letter as soon as she possibly could.

My dear Niece,

I have just received your letter and shall devote this morning to answering it. I must confess myself surprised by your application. I assumed Mr. Darcy would have told you.

A few days after your father left London, Mr. Darcy called on Mr. Gardiner. He told him that he had traced Wickham to a lodging house and had found Wickham gone and Lydia injured. He had taken her to Pemberley to recover. After a few weeks, he transferred her to a location in London.

He apologized for not letting us know of her location earlier, but he was most concerned for her health and told us that he felt the need to take care of her immediately.

His other motive was to make amends for the wrongs Wickham had done. He felt in some way responsible. He said if he had not been so proud, if he had let Wickham's worthlessness be known, no young woman of character would have been tempted by him.

If he had any other motives, I am sure it would never disgrace him.

Mr. Gardiner tried to reimburse him for his costs, but Mr. Darcy refused. He insisted on paying all of her expenses, for all the servants hired for her care.

He continues to search for Wickham, but so far has been unsuccessful.

As for Lydia, she was weak for a long time, but she has been uncharacteristically calm and happy. In some ways, she reminds me more of Jane than her usual self. But then again, I believe she has learned from her experience. She has apologized often, expressing regret for her foolish actions that led her to trust Wickham.

I hope that her reunion has been a happy one and that she can resume her life in Meryton with more wisdom.

You may be cross with me, but I must take this opportunity of saying how much I like your Mr. Darcy.

At this, Elizabeth put the letter down. Not my Mr. Darcy, she thought, but admitted that she wished he could be hers. She continued to read.

His behaviour to us has, in every respect, been as pleasing as it was in Derbyshire. His understanding and opinions all please me, he wants nothing but a little more liveliness and that, if he marries prudently, his wife may teach him. I thought him very sly. He hardly ever mentioned your name. But slyness seems the fashion. Pray forgive me, if I have been very presuming, or at least do not punish me so far as to exclude me from P. I shall never be quite happy till I have been all the way around the park. A low phaeton, with a nice little pair of ponies would be the very thing. But I must write no more. Yours very sincerely,

M. Gardiner

Elizabeth folded the letter and held it against her heart. Darcy had sought out and cared for Lydia – a girl whom he could neither regard nor esteem. Her heart did whisper that he had done it for her. But it was a hope shortly checked by other considerations.

He did feel some responsibility for Wickham and he was a doctor, after all. Perhaps he saw taking care of Lydia as more of an obligation, rather than a choice.

If he really cared for her, why did he not come with Lydia when she returned? Or why had he not come to visit Netherfield with Mr. Bingley? It appeared he was actively avoiding Longbourn and her.

CHAPTER EIGHTEEN

One morning, about two weeks after Bingley's engagement with Jane had been formed and a week since Lydia's return, as the females of the family were sitting together in the dining room, their attention was suddenly drawn to the window by the sound of a carriage; and they perceived a chaise and four driving up the lawn. It was too early in the morning for visitors, and the equipage did not look like any of their neighbours. When the door was thrown open, Elizabeth saw that it was Lady Catherine de Bourgh.

She announced this to her mother and sisters and they were all surprised.

Lady Catherine came into the dining room with an ungracious air and sat down without saying a word.

Mrs. Bennet received her with politeness, but Lady Catherine's air was one of cool civility. After several minutes, she announced, "Miss Bennet, there seems to be a prettyish kind of a wilderness on one side of your lawn. I should be glad to take a turn in it, if you will favour me with your company."

"Go, my dear," her mother urged. "And show her ladyship about the different walks."

Elizabeth obeyed.

As soon as they were both outside, Lady Catherine began. "You can be at no loss, Miss Bennet to understand the reason of my journey hither. Your own heart, your own conscience, must tell you why I have come."

"Indeed, you are mistaken."

"Do not trifle with me. I was told, that not only your sister was on the point of being most advantageously married, but that you, that Miss Elizabeth Bennet, would, in all likelihood be soon afterwards united to my nephew, Mr. Darcy. Though I know it must be a scandalous falsehood, I instantly resolved on setting off for this place that I might make my sentiments known to you."

"If you believed it impossible," Elizabeth said, colouring with astonishment. "I wonder you took the trouble of coming so far. What could your ladyship propose by it?"

"To insist upon having such a report universally contradicted."

"Your coming to Longbourn, to see me and my family will be rather a confirmation of it; if, indeed such a report is in existence."

"Do not toy with me, Miss Bennet. Has my nephew made you an offer of marriage?"

"Your ladyship has declared it to be impossible."

"And it should be so. He should marry my daughter, but you have used your wiles to gain his affection. I should have noticed when you were at Rosings, but it seemed so improbable that he could choose you over Anne, given your inferior birth and connections."

Elizabeth was reminded of Mr. Darcy's proposal. He had been correct in thinking that his family would not approve of her. She responded, "It is Mr. Darcy's choice whether my birth is adequate."

"If you marry him, you will be censured, slighted and despised by everyone connected with him. Your alliance will be a disgrace. Your name will never even be mentioned by any of us."

"Those are heavy misfortunes," Elizabeth replied. "But nothing in comparison to the happiness of being the wife of Mr. Darcy."

"Then you are determined to have him."

It was too late for that. Elizabeth said, "I have said no such thing. I am only resolved to act in that manner, which will, in my own opinion constitute my happiness, without reference to you, or to any person so wholly unconnected with me."

Lady Catherine said, "If you do marry him, you will not be happy. I warn you. He takes after his father. He is obsessed with science and medicine. Just like his father, he will put his pursuits, his interests before you. His father's selfishness broke my sister's heart."

For a moment, Elizabeth's heart was touched by the obvious sincerity in Lady Catherine's words. "If your ladyship thinks that, why would you want your daughter to marry him?"

"She has been brought up to accept his nature. She will not expect from him what he cannot give." Lady Catherine said, "Why can you not accept the fact that she is meant for him and abandon your pursuit?"

"I am not the source of your unhappiness, Lady Catherine. Mr. Darcy is his own man. If he wants to marry your daughter, he will. If not, he won't. And nothing either of us say or do will make a jot of difference." Even as she spoke, the words felt like her own death sentence.

Lady Catherine considered her comments for a moment, then sniffed. "These are your final words on the subject?"

"Yes, your ladyship."

Lady Catherine said, "Then I will go. I take no leave of you, Miss Bennet. I send no compliments to your mother. You deserve no such attention. I am most seriously displeased."

As am I, Elizabeth thought sadly.

* * *

The days finally passed and the day approached for Jane and Bingley's wedding. Bingley's sisters arrived from Town, as well as Mr. Darcy, who planned to stay the night and leave immediately after the wedding.

"That sounds ideal to me," Mrs. Bennet said. "I am glad I do not have to spend more than a few hours being polite to him."

Elizabeth was embarrassed, knowing how much Darcy had done for them by saving Lydia's life.

At the wedding, he looked silent, grave and indifferent. Elizabeth could not determine how he felt for her. Obviously he had come to the wedding for Bingley's sake, but what did he feel for her? If he no longer cared for her, why was he silent? He was still infuriating, and she was torn, not knowing if she should approach him.

At the wedding breakfast, she summoned her courage to speak to him. "Mr. Darcy, I am glad you could come for the wedding."

"Yes, I would not miss it."

"Do you agree now that my sister loves Mr. Bingley?"

He glanced in their direction. Bingley was handsome in his wedding finery and Jane was radiant in a gown of blue. "Yes, I was wrong about her before. I sincerely wish both Mr. and Mrs. Bingley every happiness."

Again he was silent, then he looked away. "Mr. Darcy," Elizabeth said. "I sense that you do not wish to talk with me, but there is something I must say, even if it pains you."

"Is there something wrong?" he asked. "Are you ill?"

She smiled. He was a doctor and would always think first of her health. "No. Only that I can no longer help thanking you for your kindness to my poor sister. Ever since I have known it, I have been most anxious to acknowledge to you how grateful I am. Were it known to the rest of my family, I should not have merely my own gratitude to express."

"No thanks are necessary. I only acted to make restitution for the harm caused by Wickham."

"You are not responsible for his actions."

"Perhaps not, but as you once said, my father was. And when he died, he left that responsibility to me. As much as I hate the fact, Wickham is still my brother."

"I spoke hastily before. Forgive me. I don't believe your father is to blame for Wickham, either. We are all of us responsible for our own actions. And I do thank you for caring for Lydia."

"You might not thank me if you knew the truth."

His serious tone made her pause. "And what is it?"

Darcy said, "Not in here. If I am to tell you the truth, we must do it privately."

Elizabeth walked with him to the gardens outside. "You begin to frighten me, Mr. Darcy."

"I frighten myself." Together they walked beyond view of the house into a small park. Elizabeth sat on a stone bench and he sat beside her. Darcy said, "When I found your sister, she was dead by Wickham's hand. The guilt and sorrow I felt threatened to overcome me, and I resolved to bring her back to her family, whole once more."

She gasped.

"Yes. I took her body to Pemberley and reanimated her."

"But how? How did you manage it without the watchmen discovering it?"

"I bribed the landlady. She did not mind, for she did not want it known that there had been a murder in her establishment. Then Greenwood and I conveyed Lydia's body to Pemberley."

Elizabeth sensed that the matter was much more complicated than he made it appear now.

He continued, "We had to work at night. Mrs. Reynolds was the only one who knew, and even she does not know all the particulars. As it was, I had to replace your sister's heart because Wickham had damaged it beyond repair."

She thought of Miss King. "Did he stab her?"

He nodded.

Elizabeth shuddered to think of his murderous rage. "Poor Lydia."

"He had strangled her before that, so she did not feel it."

Elizabeth put a hand to her throat, remembering Wickham's attempt on her. "Where did you find a replacement heart?"

"I had purchased two other corpses while in London, to use as parts if necessary, but when I came to Pemberley, I learnt of the death of Mrs. Barker, Pemberley's pastry cook. She had died peacefully in her sleep of old age. She was a kind woman, and I thought it better to use her heart rather than that of a stranger. Can you forgive me?"

"Forgive you? You gave us Lydia again."

"I know, and now I question myself. It seemed right at the time, but once she was alive again, I began to fear. What if she became like Wickham?"

"No," Elizabeth said. "How can she be like Wickham? She is already better than she was before. She is happier and kinder. Calmer. Whether that is from her improved heart or her experiences, I don't know. But you must not torment yourself. You acted out of compassion."

"I won't do it again," he said. "I don't know how my father lived with himself. I feel like Asclepius waiting for the wrath of Zeus."

"Then let it be done. Finished."

"It is not done as long as Wickham roams the earth. I have spent the past weeks searching for him, following every trail. I only came to Longbourn for Bingley's wedding."

"And not for me?" Elizabeth asked looking deep into his eyes and blushing at her boldness. "Not even a little bit?"

Darcy drew his breath in sharply. "Elizabeth, you are too generous to tease me. Don't let me dream of what can never be. If your feelings are still what they were last April, tell me so at once. My affections and wishes are unchanged, but one word from you will silence me on this subject forever."

Elizabeth felt the awkwardness and anxiety of his situation and forced herself to speak. "My feelings have changed completely."

CASS GRIX

She had never seen him look so hopeful. "Then you will marry me?"

She had been thinking about this for days, thinking it could never happen. But she knew what she wanted. "Yes, I will."

He smiled with heartfelt delight, then caught her up in his arms and kissed her once, then twice, then leaned back and laughed at their mutual breathlessness.

"Oh, Elizabeth," he said joyfully.

"Oh Frankenstein?" she said, and laughed as well. "I still think of you as Mr. Darcy."

"Frank," he said. "Only my father called me Frankenstein." At the mention of his father, his countenance changed. "There is something else you need to know."

Elizabeth steeled herself.

Darcy took her hands in his. "When I told you I was not one of my father's experiments, I was mistaken. I did not know the entire truth."

For a moment Elizabeth felt a wave of fear, but then she reminded herself that Darcy had already proven himself to her. She loved him as he was. "Yes?" she prompted.

"When I was shot, I died. My father replaced some of my intestines and reanimated me."

"So it is only your digestive system that is new. You don't have uneven arms or something like that?"

"You noticed that on Greenwood?"

"Yes, it took a while for me to discern the difference, but I was aware that something was not quite right."

He nodded. "You are observant. That is one of the things I like about you."

"But the rest of you is in one piece."

"Yes."

Elizabeth said calmly, "That does not bother me at all."

Darcy said, "You are not afraid that I will become like Wickham?"

"Why would I? Greenwood is a perfectly gentle man, no worse for his surgeries. No, I think Wickham is different. You said he had vicious tendencies as a child."

"He did. I believe the surgeries and re-animation may have augmented those tendencies."

"Did you change after your surgery?" she asked.

"Some," he admitted. "I trusted the world less and became more guarded."

"That seems reasonable, considering that someone tried to kill you. I have changed, too, since Wickham tried to strangle me. I startle at sudden noises and I no longer go walking by myself."

Darcy said, "It was worse for me. I have been a selfish being all my life, in practice, though not in principle. As a child I was taught what was right, but I was not taught to correct my temper. I was given good principles, but left to follow them in pride and conceit. I was spoilt by my parents, who though good themselves, allowed me to be selfish and overbearing. I cared for none beyond my own family and thought meanly of the rest of the world."

"No, you are too harsh on yourself. You would not have become a physician if you did not care for your fellow man."

"Perhaps not, but I still thought myself better than the rest of the world. And such I was at eight and twenty, and such I would have remained, but for you, dearest, loveliest Elizabeth. You humbled me. I came to you at Rosings without a doubt of my reception."

"I regret the harshness of my response."

"No, what did you say that I did not deserve?

"Well, let us not quarrel for the greater part of the blame for that evening. The conduct of neither of us was irreproachable, but since then, we have both, I hope, improved in civility."

He asked, "Did my letter help to change your mind?"

"It did. And my visit to Pemberley. I am almost

afraid of what you thought of me when you first saw me."

"I was thrilled. My object, then, was to show you that I did not resent the past, and I hoped to obtain your forgiveness, to lessen your ill opinion, by letting you see that your reproofs had been attended to. As to when I knew I was still in love with you? Possibly five minutes later."

Elizabeth smiled. "It took me a little longer, I am afraid. I knew I liked you, but I did not know that I loved you until I thought I had lost you, after Lydia's elopement."

"Which brings us back to where we began today." He glanced at Longbourn. Some of the wedding guests were now milling outside. "Must we go back? I wish we could elope ourselves."

Elizabeth said, "We must say good bye to Jane and Bingley."

"And I will speak to your father to get his permission." He sighed. "And as much as I would like to marry quickly, I must bring Wickham to justice first. He may have gone to Scotland. He was born there. Some of his mother's family is still there."

Elizabeth knew that Darcy would not rest until Wickham paid for his misdeeds. "I hope you find him quickly," she said and was rewarded with a kiss.

* * *

After Mr. Bennet spoke to Darcy, he asked to speak to Elizabeth in his library. "Lizzy, what are you doing? Are you out of your senses to be accepting this man? Have you not always hated him?"

"I did at first, but I have changed my mind, and now I love him most dearly."

"So you are determined to have him. He is rich, to be sure and you may have more fine clothes and fine carriages than Jane. But will they make you happy?"

It hurt her to think that he thought she was like her mother. "Do you think so little of me?"

"No, but why else would you want him? Everyone knows he is a proud, unpleasant sort of man."

"He was the one who found Lydia and arranged for her medical care. He paid for everything."

Mr. Bennet said, "Then I am in his debt, but that does not mean he is the right man for you. I would like you to be able to esteem your husband, to look up to him."

Elizabeth blanched. "Did you refuse him?"

"No, I have given him my consent. He is the kind of man, indeed, to whom I should never dare refuse anything. I see that you are resolved on having him, but let me advise you to think better of it. Mr. Darcy did not set a date and tells me he wants to find

Wickham first. I appreciate his motives and I am glad because it will give you more time to reconsider his proposal."

Mr. Bennet added, "Do not tell your mother. Keep your engagement secret until closer to the wedding. Then if you decide to cry off, there will be less scandal."

"I won't cry off," Elizabeth promised.

"Time will tell," Mr. Bennet said, and patted her hand. "I gave him permission to write to me, and I will forward his letters to you. That way, you can correspond without giving rise to gossip."

"Thank you, Papa," she said gratefully. "I believe you will come to like him once you know him better."

"That will be a first," Mr. Bennet said dryly. "Usually I like people less as I get to know them."

* * *

Darcy was gone for two months. During that time, Elizabeth felt as if she was in a dream. She went about her daily life, thinking of her secret. When Darcy returned, she would marry him, but until then, she must pretend to be her usual self.

His letters opened his heart to her. He spoke of his attempts to find Wickham and she read that he was a man tormented by regrets and yet he was relentless in his pursuit. But he also wrote of his desire for her and the happiness they would share when the evil that was Wickham was over. They wrote of books and ideas and Elizabeth felt as if she had found the friend she had always craved, as well as the lover.

She told him of her conversation with Lady Catherine, but he assured her that her fears were groundless. "I don't care what my family thinks, for you will be my family."

Finally, she received a letter that answered her prayers:

Dearest Elizabeth,

I hope this letter finds you well. And yes, I speak as your doctor as well as your future husband.

I am pleased to write that our long wait is over. I will soon return to London where I will obtain a special license and then you can name the day when Miss Bennet will become Mrs. Darcy.

As I wrote before, I travelled to Ireland to find Wickham. But I learned that the boat that left Portsmouth, the one carrying him, sank off the coast of Cork with no survivors. Although I have sympathy for the other passengers and their families, I could not help but rejoice in the neatness of Heaven's plan. George Wickham no longer roams the earth, destroying others in his greed and anger. He is gone and we may now live at peace.

I feel like a new man, full of hope for the future. I did not realize before how greatly Wickham's actions weighed upon my mind. Now that he is dead, I feel more hopeful than I have in years.

I have so many plans for the hospital in London that I fear you will think me as obsessed as my father. But believe me, that you and God willing, one day our family, will come first.

I am impatient to see you again, to take you in my arms and kiss you as I did before I left.

Dream of me, Elizabeth.

I will return as quickly as I can.

Forever yours,

FD

Elizabeth kissed the letter, wishing the author were there before her.

She first spoke to her father, then told her mother, who sat down on a chair and demanded her smelling salts. "Good gracious! Mr. Darcy? Who would have thought it? And you've been writing to him all this time? And your father has already given his permission? Oh, I don't know if my nerves can stand the excitement."

She covered her heart with her hand and said in a

lower voice, "I have heard some strange tales about the Darcy family, you know how people love to gossip, but I don't care if some say he is one of the walking dead. For ten thousand pounds a year, you could marry a corpse."

"Mama," Elizabeth said. "That is all nonsense. Lies from Mr. Wickham."

"To be sure," her mother said, smiling again. "Ten thousand pounds a year. What pin-money, what jewels, what carriages you will have! Jane's is nothing to it. I am so pleased. Such a charming man. So handsome and so tall. I hope he won't remember how much I disliked him. Do you think he noticed?"

"I think he will forgive all in the happiness of marrying me," Elizabeth said honestly.

"Oh," Mrs. Bennet said. "How soon will you want to wed? Mr. Bennet is so vexing. He should have told me sooner so we could buy the wedding attire. I don't want a rushed wedding."

I do, Elizabeth thought immodestly, but did not say it. Her only prayer now was that Frankenstein Darcy would travel in safety and return to her.

CHAPTER NINETEEN

On her wedding day, Elizabeth woke early and walked out into the gardens at Longbourn. It was chilly, so she wore a shawl over her nightgown. Her slippers became damp with dew. She watched the rising sun, and thought of Darcy, who was staying at Netherfield.

She was surprised to see a tall figure walking towards her. It was Darcy. He must have come the three miles from Netherfield. He wore a great coat and boots, but his shirt was open at the neck, without a cravat. He had not shaved and there was a fine stubble across his cheeks and jaw.

She stood, watching him with a smile on her face. "If you are coming to warn me that you have changed your mind, I will not be happy."

He smiled in response. "No, I came because I wanted to speak to you privately before the noise and confusion of the day. You mentioned in a letter that you often walked in the gardens at sunrise, and I hoped to meet you."

"I should not have been so open in my letters. I fear you know all my secrets, now."

"I doubt that," he said and kissed her hand. "There are a few left."

Elizabeth blushed at his obvious meaning but kept her gaze steady on his handsome face. How she loved him. She breathed deeply, savouring his familiar scent. She began to think that peppermint would become an aphrodisiac to her. "Are you not worried? They say it is bad luck for the groom to see the bride on the wedding day."

"I don't believe in superstitions," he said. "Remember, I am a man of science."

"Yes, Dr. Darcy."

He smiled and touched her hair, teasing one riotous curl by her ear. "Have I told you that I love you?"

"Not sufficiently," she said pertly, which prompted another kiss, this on her lips.

After a few moments, he withdrew from her with a sigh. "Ah, Miss Bennet," he said. "We do not want to get ahead of ourselves."

She straightened her shawl. "No, time enough for all that this evening."

"This afternoon," he corrected with a gleam in his eye.

Elizabeth laughed. Her mother had warned her about the duties of the marriage bed, but instead of horrifying her, the explanations had only intrigued her. Judging from the way she felt whenever her fiancé kissed her, she deduced that it would be quite exciting to become Mrs. Darcy.

He smiled, then his expression changed and became more serious. "I would spend the rest of the morning talking with you, if I could, but the servants are already waking and I don't want your father to catch us."

"Then please, tell me what you wished to say."

He nodded. He motioned to the scar across his throat. "You have seen this already. But you haven't seen this." He started to untuck his loose white shirt from his pantaloons.

"It is not necessary," Elizabeth protested but he then bared his stomach. There was a neat pink angular line across his abdomen. She had known that he was physically fit, but she was surprised by the definition of his muscles.

"Will you take this scarred, imperfect man?" he asked.

Elizabeth felt as if her heart was beating in her throat and tears filled her eyes. She placed one tender hand on his abdomen and reached up to kiss the scar on his throat. "Yes," she said solemnly. "For I am imperfect as well."

* * *

Later that evening, Darcy prepared for bed at Darcy House. They had driven to London after the wedding, with plans to stay there several days and then go on a tour in the North. Elizabeth was already in her bedroom with her new lady's maid Fisk. Darcy thought about the day, remembering their wedding. As much as he had enjoyed seeing Elizabeth in her finery, vowing before God and man to cherish and love him until death parted them, he thought he would value their private vows that morning even more.

Part of him could not believe that the fear and effort of the past few months were over, that Wickham was safely dead. He was pleased with Lydia's recovery. She seemed healthy and as Elizabeth said, she was more calm, although not above teasing Elizabeth as they prepared to leave.

He would never forget the parting words of Mr. Bennet. "I have given you a jewel, Mr. Darcy. Take care of her."

Darcy changed into a night shirt and donned a silk robe, tied at the waist. He knocked gently on the adjoining door.

There was a moment of silence, then Elizabeth said in a strained voice. "Come in."

He smiled, wondering if she was as nervous as he.

But when he opened the door, he saw Wickham, holding Elizabeth by her hair, with a knife at her throat.

"Let go of my wife," Darcy said and started to rush towards him, but Wickham ordered, "Stand back if you value her life."

Darcy stilled, his mind racing, considering his options. If only he had a weapon – a knife or a pistol – but he had nothing.

"I am sorry," Elizabeth said to Darcy, but Wickham said, "Make one more sound and I kill you now. Understood?"

Elizabeth nodded, her eyes wide.

Wickham looked like a madman, his clothes worn and dirty, his hair long.

Darcy said, "Why are you doing this?"

"I am malicious because I am miserable."

"What can you hope to gain?"

"Justice. Why should you find a wife for your bosom, and yet I be alone? Why should you be happy while I grovel in the intensity of my wretchedness? You may hate me, but I will have my revenge, which is dearer than light or food! I may die, but first you will curse the sun that gazes on your misery. I am fearless, which makes me more powerful than you."

Darcy said, "You'll hang."

"Maybe," Wickham agreed. "But I have the devil's own luck. And if not, I will disappoint the Resurrection Men." He laughed. "How annoyed they will be to find that parts of my body have been twice used." He pressed the blade into Elizabeth's neck and she flinched. Silent tears ran down her face. Wickham said, "Now close the door behind you and lock it."

Darcy obeyed, being careful not to turn his back to Wickham.

"Throw me the key," Wickham said.

Darcy tossed the key so that it landed by Wickham's feet, but Wickham did not bend down to pick it up.

"You will never get out of here alive," Darcy said clearly.

"And this time, I don't have your father to patch me up. Not that it matters. After all I've done? I am polluted by my crimes and torn by the bitterest remorse. Where can I find rest but in death?"

Darcy saw that Wickham was oddly excited, eager to talk. He hoped that if he could keep him talking, he would find a way to reach for a log from the fire. He asked, "Why did you kill Lydia?"

Wickham seemed surprised by the question. "That was a mistake. I did not mean to kill her, just to frighten her a little, to punish her for laughing at me, but she struggled."

"And you killed her." Darcy could not keep the contempt from his voice.

"I know you hate me," Wickham said. "But your abhorrence cannot equal that with which I regard myself. I liked Lydia. I did not mean to hurt her."

"You have remorse now. But what about Mary King?"

"She ended our engagement and was going to marry Denny instead. I had to stop her."

"And her uncle?"

"He heard her cry out and came into the room."

"You always have an excuse," Darcy said.

As Wickham spoke, he relaxed his hold on Elizabeth slightly. She tried to pull away, but he caught her back again and in the process, the blade actually nicked her skin.

Elizabeth cried out, but then silenced. A stream of blood trickled down her white throat.

"I will do the job correctly this time," Wickham said to her.

Darcy took one step towards the fireplace.

Wickham then spoke to Darcy calmly, as if they were sitting across a dining room table. "You might not realize it, but it is rather difficult to kill someone by slitting their throat."

"You," Darcy said with astonishment. "You were

the one who attacked me in London?"

Wickham laughed. "Who else?"

"But why?"

"The money of course, but after you managed to live, I thought it poetic justice that you were scarred like I was. I hoped you'd understand how I felt."

"You are mad," Darcy said.

"Angry," Wickham corrected. "What right did our father have to bring me back to life? He made me into a circus freak."

Darcy glanced briefly at the fireplace. "Your scars are hardly noticeable. No one would know the truth, if you did not tell them."

"I knew the truth, and I hated him for it. Just as I have always hated you."

"What did I ever do to you?"

"You were born to be Master of Pemberley and I was not."

Darcy had no answer for that. With one quick motion, he reached for a burning stick and threw it at Wickham's face.

Wickham ducked and staggered back. "Damn you," he cried and momentarily loosened his hold on Elizabeth, who pulled free and ran back to the corner of the room.

Darcy took a step towards Wickham, to bring him

down, but Wickham swung the knife before himself in a horizontal arc. "Stay back," he ordered.

Elizabeth handed Darcy a poker from the fire.

"Excellent," Darcy said. He balanced the weight of it in his hand. It was not a sabre, but it would have to do. He crouched slightly and stepped closer. Out of the corner of his eye, he saw that Elizabeth had picked up a chair as well. She was magnificent in her anger with her dark hair wild about her shoulders, her nightgown pale in the candlelight. Together they would be able to contain him.

"You think you've won," Wickham said. "But I have the upper hand. I am still my own person, not our father's creature. I will choose when I die, Brother, not you." And with that, he stuck the knife into his own throat and slashed downward.

Immediately he sank to the floor.

"Is he dead?" Elizabeth asked.

"Not yet," Darcy said. He stood over him, waiting as he bled out. Within minutes, Wickham was truly dead, not breathing and with no pulse.

EPILOGUE

The sun shone on another wedding day, but instead of Hertfordshire or London, Mr. and Mrs. Darcy were in Scotland, just across the border in Gretna Green.

The groom, Greenwood, stood tall and solemn in his wedding finery.

His bride, Miss Ellis, stood beside him in a new dress of dark green with a fine white lace collar. The burn on her cheek had faded to a narrow pink oval, no larger than her finger.

Their officiator was the owner of an inn, a tall gentleman with a kindly air. According to the laws of Scotland, anyone could act as priest and the ceremony was less complex than that in England. An attestation of marriage before witnesses was sufficient.

The man wrote their names on his certificate and then asked, "Did you come here of your own free will and accord?"

Greenwood groaned.

"That is yes," Darcy said.

"A nod will be sufficient, Mr. Greenwood," the man said. "I believe the Lord looks on the heart in matters such as these."

Greenwood nodded.

"And you, Miss Ellis?" the man asked.

"Yes."

The man then asked solemnly, "Do you take this woman to be your lawful wedded wife, forsaking all others, keeping to her as long as you both shall live?"

Greenwood made a grunt and nodded.

The man turned to Miss Ellis, "Do you take this man to be your lawful wedded husband, forsaking all others, keeping to him as long as you both shall live?"

"I will."

"Very good," he said. "Is there a ring?"

Darcy produced a ring from his waistcoat pocket and Greenwood with his thick fingers, managed to place it on his wife's hand.

They then took each other by their right hands and the man announced, "What God has joined together, let no man put asunder. In as much as this man and this woman have consented to go together by giving and receiving a ring, I therefore, declare them to be man and wife."

At this point, congratulations and kisses were exchanged. Darcy was happy for Greenwood, but he watched Elizabeth. How beautiful she was with the light shining on her dark hair.

As Greenwood had said, she was his heart, even more so now that they had been married for almost two years. She had taught him how to love and how to put bitterness behind him.

He thought briefly of their own wedding day and Wickham's attack. So much had happened since then. After Wickham's death, Elizabeth said she thought he might have been the one who shot him at Pemberley years before and that made sense to Darcy. Darcy made further inquiries about Miss King's death and was able to clear Mr. Denny's reputation. He could not bring the man back to life, but at least it was a comfort to his family to know that he had been a hero, trying to save Elizabeth, rather than a murderer.

As for Lydia, she had visited Pemberley and fallen in love with the rector at Kympton. They were married now, which continually surprised Mrs. Bennet. "To think of Lydia, a clergyman's wife like Charlotte Lucas!"

Darcy thought it was a sort of divine justice for her to be the beneficiary of the living that had once been promised to Wickham.

In the spring, Georgiana would finally have her London Season. She was still shy, but Elizabeth had helped her gain more confidence. Darcy often reminded Georgiana not to be in a hurry to fall in love.

Jane and Bingley had bought an estate twenty miles from Pemberley but were rarely there. They were currently in Russia, preparing for an Arctic voyage. Darcy did not know how Bingley had convinced her, but Jane was now enamoured of icebergs as well.

For the past two years, he and Elizabeth had spent the majority of their time in London, where he continued to train and supervise the doctors in his small private hospital. But now with Elizabeth's recent pregnancy, he wanted to return to Pemberley. Elizabeth, knowing that he might be bored with only the estate to manage had suggested he open rooms in Lambton as well.

Sometimes it amazed him the serpentine turns his life had taken and how much happier he was now, with Elizabeth as his wife and a baby on the way. He wished his parents could have met her. He hoped that if it were possible, that they were able to look down on them from heaven.

After a few minutes, Darcy walked with his wife out into the inn's courtyard. He said, "There. I suppose Greenwood is Miss Ellis's responsibility now."

"Mrs. Greenwood," Elizabeth corrected.

"I think it was best to come to Scotland," Darcy said. "I am not certain our rector would have been as accommodating."

"No, I agree," Elizabeth said. "And it gives us a chance for a second honeymoon, as well."

"That is right. We should spend a few days here and not make Mr. and Mrs. Greenwood hurry home. And it will be good for you to rest before travelling again."

Elizabeth smiled. "I don't need to rest. I feel perfectly fine."

"As your doctor," Darcy said, "I want you to be careful."

"You sound like your father."

He frowned. "In what way?"

"Mrs. Reynolds told me that your mother lost two children before you, both born too early."

"I did not know that."

"And your father, in his concern, was very cautious when she was expecting you. As soon as he learned that her courses were delayed, he refused to leave her side, not even to go to Lambton. I hope you will not be quite as strict with me."

"I don't think that will be necessary," Darcy began, then startled. "Are you saying he never left Pemberley?"

"No, not even for a day. Mrs. Reynolds found it extraordinary. Apparently he did the same before Georgiana was born."

Darcy could not believe what he was hearing. If his father never left Pemberley, he could not have fathered Wickham. It was a physical impossibility. Wickham's mother had been in Scotland. But his father had confessed on his deathbed – or had he?

Darcy tried to remember his actual words. That Wickham was a second son to him or like a second son? He had been speaking so softly, had Darcy misunderstood him?

And the guilt his father felt, that could easily be explained by his going against his wife's wishes.

Dear God, Darcy thought. The guilt that he had carried for years for hating a member of his own family slipped from him, washed away as if taken by a tide. If Wickham was not his half-brother, he did not need to second guess himself, wondering whether his failure to give Wickham more money had led to his crimes.

And his father, his dear generous father, was the man he always thought he was – not perfect but honourable.

"Frank," Elizabeth asked with concern. "Are you all right?"

Darcy looked at his beautiful, brilliant wife and

smiled. "I am fine. Better than fine. I just realized that Wickham could not be my half-brother. We were not related at all."

"I am glad to hear it," she said. "I have never known two men less similar."

She took his arm and they walked down the road, as they often walked at Pemberley. He felt like a new man with his entire life before him.

After a few minutes, she looked up at him from the corner of her eyes. "What do you suggest we do this afternoon, Mr. Darcy?" He was often Mr. Darcy when she teased him. "We are not in London, so there are no patients for you to check on."

He recognized her flirtatious tone and was pleased that he and his wife were so often of like minds. Unlike many women of their era, Elizabeth fully embraced her physical nature, meeting him passion for passion. He was a lucky man. "You decide, Mrs. Darcy. I am completely and utterly at your disposal."

She smiled. "I saw a very nice pond when we rode into town."

He pretended to be shocked. "You wish to go swimming?" They often swam at Pemberley.

"Oh, not in my condition," she said and touched the slight swell of her stomach. "I thought we could have a rock skipping contest."

"Agreed, Mrs. Darcy," he said and kissed her lightly. "And what shall be the prize?"

Her fine eyes sparkled, promising him the world. "Whatever you wish, Mr. Darcy."

The End

AUTHOR'S NOTE:

I hope you enjoyed *Frankenstein Darcy*. I enjoyed reading the original Frankenstein story by Mary Shelley as an example of Regency Era fiction, and I thought a mashup of the two would be a lot of fun.

If you liked this book, check out my other quirky Jane Austen Variations:

Stealing Darcy and *Bewitching Mr. Darcy*.

To receive a free download of *Stealing Darcy*, please go to my website and sign up for my VIP reader's group. http://cassgrix.com/sd-fd-signup2/

Finally, I love to hear from my readers. You can email me at: cass.grix.author@gmail.com

Or leave a review. I love reviews.

Thanks.

Happy reading,
Cass

Here is a bonus excerpt of *Stealing Darcy*. Armed with gypsy magic, Caroline Bingley plots to take Fitzwilliam Darcy away from Elizabeth Bennet. Caroline takes Elizabeth's place – through a body swap – and Darcy must determine which woman is his true love.

* * *

Elizabeth woke late. The household seemed unnaturally quiet. She opened her eyes and saw that she was in a different bedroom in a bed with a canopy of heavy curtains tied back. She sat up straight. There must be some mistake. Had she gone into the wrong bedroom last night after saying good night to Jane?

She didn't think she had drunk too much wine, but perhaps the strain of taking care of Jane had made her wearier and less observant. She looked about for her robe, but it was not draped over a chair as she had left it.

She saw that the fire in the fireplace had already been laid. There was a knock at the door.

"Come in?" Elizabeth said.

A maid entered, carrying a tray that she placed on a table beside the bed. There was a small pot of tea and a plate with toast. "Do you want the windows open, ma'am?"

Perhaps a little fresh air would make her think more clearly. "Yes, thank you."

The windows were opened and a clean cool breeze filled the room.

"Would you like chocolate today, ma'am?"

This was a first. No one had offered her chocolate before. "No, thank you," she said carefully. She swung her legs over the side of the bed and saw a pair of embroidered slippers that were not hers on the floor.

She then stood and saw her reflection in a large gilt mirror on the wall. But instead of her own reflection, she saw Miss Bingley in a nightdress with tousled hair.

She cried out in surprise and looked quickly back to the bed behind her, but Caroline Bingley was not there.

"Are you all right, ma'am?" the maid said.

"Yes. No. I don't know," Elizabeth said. She brought her hand up to cover the lower half of her face and in the reflection Caroline Bingley did the same.

This must be a dream. For some reason her mind had turned herself into Caroline Bingley. Her head swam.

"Are you feeling faint?"

"No." She had never fainted in her life and she was not going to start now. She sat down on the bed instead.

If this wasn't a dream, was she going mad?

The maid said timidly, "Can I help you?"

"No," Elizabeth said firmly. "Not now. Please leave."

She needed to be alone to solve the problem. The maid retreated and closed the door behind her. Elizabeth walked up to the mirror in disbelief. Somehow, she had become Caroline Bingley.

She closed her eyes and rubbed her face, but when she opened them again, it was still Caroline Bingley in the mirror.

She ran her hands down at her body – she was taller and slimmer now, with slighter curve of breast and hip.

Somehow her soul was inside Miss Bingley's body.

She sat back down on the bed. This was impossible, and yet, it had happened. She put her hand on her forehead. She did not feel feverish, but if she were truly ill, would she recognize that she was hallucinating?

"Jane," she said to herself. She would know what to do.

She hurried out into the hall, then went back into the bedroom for a robe. She hastily tied the sash about her waist and walked down the hallways to the guest bedrooms. When she got to Jane's room, a maid was making up the bed. "Is Miss Bennet here?" she asked.

"Oh no, ma'am. Both Miss Bennets are at breakfast."

Elizabeth would not be able to talk to her privately

at breakfast, dressed as she was. She returned to Caroline's room and found another maid, most likely Miss Bingley's lady's maid, waiting for her.

"Are you all right, ma'am?" the servant asked. "You have forgotten your slippers."

Elizabeth looked down at her bare feet and wiggled her toes. It was so strange to see different feet, to feel herself within a different body. But the lack of slippers was the least of her concerns.

"I must get dressed," she said.

"Yes, of course, ma'am," the woman said. "But your hair first?"

"Yes," Elizabeth said. She was not accustomed to having someone help with her hair, except perhaps when she was going to a party, but she did not want to create any suspicion, so she sat still and let the young woman arrange her hair.

It took more than twenty minutes and dozens of pins. Elizabeth had never realized how much work it took for Caroline Bingley to be presentable. After the hair, there was her face. The maid rubbed her face with a scented lotion, applied a discrete sprinkling of powder and a slightly tinted lotion for her lips. Then it was time to dress.

Elizabeth tried not to be embarrassed as the young woman helped her out of her nightdress and into her shift, then corset and petticoats. Caroline also wore an extra layer of ruffles across her chest to give the illusion of a larger bosom. As for day dresses, there were dozens to choose from. "Which would you prefer today?" the maid asked.

"I don't care," Elizabeth said. "You choose."

This took another twenty minutes, as the young woman guided the dress over her head and uplifted arms, being careful not to have the fabric touch her hair or face.

Once the dress was on, the fastening began.

Caroline wore her clothes much tighter than Elizabeth was accustomed to. She supposed it was fashionable, but she did not know how Caroline could take a deep breath or raise her arms. When Elizabeth tried to reach the back of her head, the fabric pulled tightly.

"Do you have an itch, ma'am?"

"No, I am fine," Elizabeth said and dropped her arms to her side. Finally, the woman had finished helping her.

"Is everything all right?" the servant asked.

Elizabeth glanced at her reflection. "It is fine. Thank you." She walked downstairs, cautiously, hoping to find Jane. She found both Jane and the young woman who appeared to be herself, eating breakfast. For a moment, Elizabeth was disoriented to see herself, calming talking. She silently served herself breakfast from a side table and sat down.

Mr. Darcy was there, as well as Bingley and Mrs. Hurst.

Mrs. Hurst said, "Caroline, it is not like you to be late for breakfast. You are usually an early riser."

"This morning was a little different," she said, thinking this was a vast understatement.

"I hope you are feeling well," Bingley said.

She sensed that he had some brotherly concern for her. "I am fine," she lied. She saw that the woman who appeared to be herself was watching her with interest. She assumed Caroline's soul had gone into her body.

Elizabeth turned to her sister. "Jane. Miss Bennet," she corrected. "I hope you are feeling better and that your exertions last night were not too taxing."

"No, indeed. I am quiet refreshed and think that perhaps I will go home today."

"Oh no, that's too soon," Mr. Bingley said. "I think you should be completely well before you brave the journey. Don't you agree, Caroline?"

Belatedly Elizabeth realized that they were all staring at her, waiting for her response. "Oh yes," she said, not wanting Jane to leave her alone. "I would not like your cold to get worse."

"Thank you," Jane said.

Elizabeth then addressed herself. "Miss Eliza," she said carefully. "Did you sleep well?"

"Yes." It was strange to hear her voice coming from another person.

"You had no problems?" she asked meaningfully.

"None at all." But there was a glint in her eyes that let Elizabeth know that it was Caroline Bingley inside her body. Somehow there had been an exchange, with each of them taking the other's place.

Caroline said, "The weather is so delightful this morning, I would like to take a walk. Will you join me, Jane?"

"No, I am not ready for a walk."

"Mr. Darcy, then?"

He looked pleased by her invitation, which surprised Elizabeth. He wanted to walk with her? Or more precisely, with Caroline pretending to be her?

Mr. Darcy said, "Yes. Mrs. Hurst, Miss Bingley, would you like to walk as well?"

Elizabeth said, "No, I think I will stay here with Jane."

She waited until everyone else had left the room, and then she approached her sister. "Jane, there is something I need to tell you."

"Yes, Caroline?"

Elizabeth hesitated, then gathered her courage and continued. "This is going to sound strange, but I am actually Elizabeth, Lizzy, your sister. I don't know how it happened, but this morning, when I woke up, I was in Caroline Bingley's body, as you see."

Jane frowned. "Is this a joke?"

"No, I am serious. I am your sister, and I think Caroline Bingley's soul is in my body."

Jane looked distressed. "If that is the case, what is to be done about it?"

"I don't know. I don't know how this happened."

Jane patted her hand. "Your poor dear. It must be very frightening."

"It is," Elizabeth said, relieved to be able to tell someone. "And I don't know what can be done. I suppose we should talk to Caroline when she returns from her walk."

"I think we should speak to Mr. Bingley," Jane said firmly.

Elizabeth did not know what he could do, but he might have a useful idea.

A footman was sent. Jane rose up to meet Mr. Bingley when he entered the room.

He seemed surprised. "Miss Bennet, is there a problem?"

"Yes, actually. I think your sister is not feeling well."

"Jane!" Elizabeth said. "Do you not believe me?"

"She is not herself," Jane said quietly. "And I think it is best if you speak with her privately."

"Very good, thank you," Bingley said.

Elizabeth watched with dread as Jane left the room. If her sister did not believe her, who would?

http://cassgrix.com/sd-fd-signup2/

Made in the USA
Charleston, SC
05 December 2016